THE RHYTHM OF TIME

QUESTLOVE

WITH S. A. COSBY

G. P. PUTNAM'S SONS

G. P. PUTNAM'S SONS
An imprint of Penguin Random House LLC, New York

First published in the United States of America by G. P. Putnam's Sons,
an imprint of Penguin Random House LLC, 2023

Text copyright © 2023 by Ahmir Khalib Thompson
Illustrations copyright © 2023 by Godwin Akpan

Visit us online at penguinrandomhouse.com.

Library of Congress Cataloging-in-Publication Data
Names: Questlove, author. | Cosby, S. A., author.
Title: The rhythm of time / Questlove with S. A. Cosby.
Description: New York: G. P. Putnam's Sons, 2023. | Summary: After accidentally
traveling back in time and rewriting the future, twelve-year-old best friends
Rahim and Kasia must work together to restore their timeline.
Identifiers: LCCN 2022046721 (print) | LCCN 2022046722 (ebook) |
ISBN 9780593354063 (hardcover) | ISBN 9780593354087 (ebook)
Subjects: CYAC: Time travel—Fiction. | Best friends—Fiction. |
Friendship—Fiction. | African Americans—Fiction.
Classification: LCC PZ7.1.Q35 Rh 2023 (print) | LCC PZ7.1.Q35 (ebook) | DDC [Fic]—dc23
LC record available at https://lccn.loc.gov/2022046721
LC ebook record available at https://lccn.loc.gov/2022046722

Printed in the United States of America
ISBN 9780593354063
1st Printing

LSCH

Design by Tony Sahara
Text set in Dante MT Std Medium

I dedicate this adventure to nine-year-old
Ahmir Khalib Thompson—a curious kid who
should follow all of his dreams.

—Questlove

To all the kids who dare to dream in color.

—S. A. Cosby

THE DAY RAHIM REYNOLDS received the gift that would change his life forever was pretty much like every other day. He went to school. He played chess on a real chessboard with Harris, one of his few friends, during lunch. He helped Mrs. Lewis in the library and picked up two Stephen King novels. During his last class, he wrote three new complete rhymes in his notebook.

And he tried to avoid Demarcus "Man Man" Richards at all costs.

Demarcus and his two sidekicks, Lavell and Tron, enjoyed three things: uploading their awful homemade raps on SoundCloud, causing trouble in class, and picking on Rahim. When the last bell rang, Rahim headed out the door with his head down and the hood on his jacket up. Harris was waiting for him on the front steps.

"You look like a glitch in the new *Assassin's Creed* patch," Harris said. Harris was tall and gangly with thick glasses and a sharp sense of humor. Rahim thought that, in any other school, Harris would be the focus of a bully like Man Man, but for some reason, Rahim took up all of Demarcus's attention. The cold February wind smacked him in the face as he stopped and gave Harris a light shoulder check.

"I've never played that game," Rahim said.

"Yeah, but you've heard of it, right? Oh, wait, I forgot," Harris said.

"Yeah, I've heard of it. Just never played it. You know my dad has a grudge against gaming. And social media and computers and—"

Harris held up his hand. "Geez, you're making me depressed."

Rahim laughed. "I gotta get going."

"You don't wanna wait for my mom? She can give you a ride. It's cold as a snowman's butt," Harris said.

Rahim laughed again. "I mean, if she don't—"

"Where you think you going, chunkbutt?"

Rahim didn't bother turning around. He knew it was Man Man. Instead, he took off at a full sprint. He heard one of the teachers yell something at Man Man and his boys, but it got lost in the wind. Rahim ducked around people making their way up the sidewalk. But he could hear Man Man's heavy footfalls closing in on him. At the last second, he cut across the street. He missed getting hit by a garbage truck by a matter of inches, but that slowed down Man Man and his sidekicks just enough for Rahim to lose them as he slipped down the alley between Mr. Daniels's corner store and the used bookstore run by Mrs. Rollins. He heard Mrs. Rollins holler something at him from her front stoop, but he was still in fight-or-flight mode and flight was in full control. He cut across another street even as the WALK/DON'T WALK sign was in the middle of changing. He passed Mr. Carlson's sandwich shop. The scent of fresh cheesesteaks almost made him slow his stride but he was close to home and couldn't take a chance on Man Man and his cronies catching up with him. He slowed to a trot as he cut through another alleyway and the gray one-eyed cat that lived there hissed at him before scurrying behind an old couch. He emerged from the alley and stepped out onto the street where he lived.

Rahim had never lived anywhere but Philly, and he had never lived anywhere in Philly except this street. No matter how bad Man Man picked on him or how lost he felt navigating the many social circles that excluded him at school, coming home always made him feel safe. This was his neighborhood. He knew these streets, these sidewalks, these street signs. This was home.

Rahim bounded up the front steps of his house. When he came through the front door, he saw his father sitting in his recliner with a heavy leather-bound book in his hands. Rahim tried closing the door softly, but the wind caught it and slammed it hard against the frame.

"We *walk* in this house, Rahim. You never need to run in a place you call home." Rahim stopped in his tracks.

"Yes, sir." He slid off his backpack and hung up his coat.

"The door," his dad said. Rahim rolled his eyes. He went back outside, came in again, and shut the door so softly it barely made a sound when it met the frame. Rahim pulled his copy of *The Tommyknockers* out of his book bag.

"How was your day?" his dad asked.

"It was okay."

"It was more than okay, since you don't seem to have any homework. That can be the only reason you are about to start that drivel instead of doing your assignments."

"But you're reading," Rahim said.

"My assignment is my reading. I'm giving my class a test on the reign of Haile Selassie tomorrow. So I'm reacquainting myself with some of the more interesting aspects of his life."

Rahim sighed. "I need to go next door and borrow Kasia's laptop. I do have to write a one-page report for social studies," he said.

Dad cleared his throat. "We have a complete set of

reference materials here, Rahim. There is no need for you to turn your brain to mush searching every single thing online."

"Dad, don't your students use the internet?" he asked.

"Yes, and you should see how lost they are when the Wi-Fi goes down and they can't reach their online oracle. I don't want you to find yourself in a college class one day with that same deer-in-the-headlights look on your face."

"We are the only people I know who don't have their own computer. You don't even like using the one the college gave you," Rahim said.

"You have to know how to crawl before you can walk, son. The internet makes it too easy for you. It's like giving you a pilot's license when you don't even know how to ride a bicycle."

Rahim's dad hadn't raised his head from his book once, but Rahim knew his dad knew he was rolling his eyes again. He was just observant like that. A slim man with dark brown skin and an unruly Afro that he refused to cut or comb, he had been a tenured history professor longer than Rahim had been alive.

"Omar, let that boy go next door. The internet might give him the information, but it ain't gonna write the paper for him." Rahim's mother was coming downstairs from her studio, where she gave violin and cello lessons to kids from all the surrounding neighborhoods. His mom always looked regal to Rahim, even when she was just helping Dad make dinner. Long, thick loc'd braids ran down her back like a waterfall.

"I'm just trying to teach him to not depend on technological contrivances."

"I know you are, honey, but the world is constantly changing. It doesn't hurt to keep up, dear."

"I wish it wasn't," Dad grumbled.

"Can I go next door?" Rahim asked. His parents could go on like this for hours. His older sister, Yasmine, said it was the opposite of an argument. She called it a loveument.

"Yes," his mother said, "but just get what you need for your assignment. Don't let Kasia talk you into being her guinea pig again. Took you two weeks to get your eyes back to normal after her X-ray glasses experiment. Carry your book bag upstairs before you go."

Rahim grabbed his backpack and headed upstairs. As he passed his sister's room, he heard her vocal exercises. His sister could hit notes that could break glass. Yasmine was like a perfect combination of Mom and Dad. She loved music like their mom, and she loved history like their dad. Rahim figured that was why she wanted to sing opera. Best of both worlds.

Before he got to his room, Yasmine opened her door and leaned into the hallway.

"Hey, bighead. You know my choir concert is this weekend, right?" Yasmine asked. She took a sip from a teacup. Rahim could smell the strong aromas coming from the cup from three feet away. Yasmine never drank sodas, never ate spicy foods, and never ever yelled. She was always trying to take care of her voice.

"Yeah, I know."

"You coming, right?" Yasmine asked.

"Well, I don't have anything else to do," Rahim said. Yasmine rolled her eyes.

"It's my first time singing lead. So it's kind of a big deal," Yasmine said.

"I'm just teasing, you know I'm going to be there. I'll even clap really loud when you hit a high note," Rahim said.

"Please just clap . . . in a regular way. Don't embarrass me," Yasmine said. She smiled at Rahim, shook her head, and closed her door.

Rahim dropped off his book bag and then slipped down the stairs and out the back door to Kasia's house. He knocked on the door three times before her mom opened it with a flourish.

"Rahim! Do you know that means 'merciful'? Mercy, mercy me!" Kasia's mom asked. She said this every time he came over. It was her favorite joke. She must have thought it was Rahim's too.

"Yes, Mrs. Collins." Unlike his parents, Kasia's parental units embraced every aspect of technology. Their house was nearly fully automated through virtual assistant technology. The home-security system was connected to each of their cell phones. They could order groceries from a touchscreen on their fridge. (Kasia had hacked it so she could order pizza without her parents—both vegans—knowing it.) If there was a new piece of tech that was supposed to make life easier, either the Collins family would buy it or Kasia would build it.

"One day you're going to get that joke and laugh yourself silly. Kasia's upstairs. Did you want to stay for dinner? Her dad is making vegetarian chili and . . . we've got rutabaga pie for dessert!" Rahim wasn't sure what a rutabaga was, but it didn't sound like any dessert he wanted.

"No, ma'am. I just need to use Kasia's computer."

"All right, but let me know if you change your mind. The crust on the pie is homemade. No premade stuff here. Oh, and tell your parents we're just about to harvest our bok choy and beets. So there will be a sale on winter veggies at the co-op," Mrs. Collins said.

"I will. What is bok choy?" Rahim asked.

"It's like an Asian cabbage. You'll love it. It's one of our biggest sellers. It actually tastes better than brussels sprouts," Mrs. Collins said.

Rahim didn't say anything. He didn't want to tell Mrs. Collins he didn't like brussels sprouts, so he probably wasn't going to like bok choy. Kasia's parents were really into veganism. They ran a company that converted unused lots into green spaces for the city. They sold a lot of the vegetables from these green spaces at a co-op in the neighborhood. The rest they donated to food banks. Yasmine like to say they were Black hipsters, whatever that was. Rahim thought they just really liked vegetables.

Rahim climbed the spiral staircase to the second floor. Kasia's parents had knocked down most of the walls upstairs to give Kasia space for her experiments. Kasia's room took up most of the second floor except for her parents' bedroom, which was toward the rear of the house. Kasia said her parents wanted her to have room to create. Rahim thought she was lucky. He barely had space to turn around in his room.

She had two huge computer monitors mounted on the wall. There was a table full of electrical equipment. Another held her chemistry equipment. Her ceiling was a map of the night sky that she and her dad had wired up themselves. When Rahim reached the top step, he saw Kasia sitting at her desk, working on her drone.

Last year she'd asked her parents for a drone, but the one she got wasn't up to her standards, so she built her own. She named him Iago.

Rahim thought Iago was named after the parrot in *Aladdin*, but Kasia said it was from a play, *Othello*, by William Shakespeare. Rahim had looked it up at the library. He'd tried to read it, but it was like it was written in another language. From what he could decipher, the ending was really sad and Iago was the bad guy.

When Rahim told her he read it, Kasia had said, "It's not sad. It's tragic. There's a difference. And Iago is not just the bad guy. He's *the* bad guy. He's the ultimate villain. And basically, he wins. It's a classic for a reason."

"If you say so," Rahim had said.

Kasia spun around on her work stool to face him. There was tape on the bridge of her glasses, but they weren't broken. Kasia called it an affectation.

"You did what I told you?"

Rahim laughed. "Yeah. I pretended I was gonna skip my homework and read my book, and my dad insisted I get right to work."

"I told you. Grab the headphones. I'll pull up the beat," Kasia said. Rahim got a pair of headphones off the table. Kasia tapped a couple of keys, and suddenly a musical computer program popped up on the bigger monitor on the wall. She reached under her desk for a wireless mic and tossed it to Rahim. She put on some headphones of her own and pointed at him. "I'm dropping the beat. Don't hesitate. Go for it!"

Rahim nodded and closed his eyes.

He thought about the rhyme he worked on in algebra class while Mr. Dudley solved for *x*. *That's a good title,* he'd thought.

> *This one's called Solve for X*
> *I'm a problem for the weak-minded*
> *You looking for the answer? You won't find it*
> *I'm more complex than E = mc²*
> *You don't want none, son, go home so*
> *You can be safe and scared*
> *You ain't got the skills*
> *You lack the education*
> *The lyrical formation*
> *You need an entire nation*
> *To solve this equation.*

Rahim stopped and caught his breath.

"Was that all freestyle?" Kasia asked.

"Yeah . . . no, kinda," Rahim said.

"Either way, it was fire," Kasia said. "Do you know what $E = mc^2$ actually means?"

"Nah. But I read about it in a sci-fi book once."

Kasia shook her head and sighed. "Short version: It means matter can't be created or destroyed. Hey, you should use that in your next song. Anyway, I'll mix it and post it tonight. You should really make a profile and post it yourself."

"So Man Man can be even madder at me? I don't think so," Rahim said. He poked Iago. "You give him any new upgrades?" Rahim asked. The little drone was more like a pet than a robot.

Kasia picked up a remote and touched a button and Iago whirred to life, flying around the second floor. "I installed an echolocation emitter on him. Now Iago can guide himself."

"Are you ever gonna do anything with him?" Rahim put the mic and headphones on the worktable.

"Like what?" Kasia asked.

"Like sell him? You know, for money?" Rahim said.

"I didn't build Iago for money."

"Let me sell him, then," he said.

"Are you ever gonna put out another song under your own name?" Kasia asked.

"I already told you: I don't need to give Man Man another reason to hate me."

"It ain't your fault everyone liked your song better than his."

"It was just my luck to post a song the same day as Man Man. I didn't even know Demarcus was Lil Kid D until he shoved me into my locker the next day."

"His name is Demarcus, he makes you call him Man Man, and he tries to rap under the name Lil Kid D. He got three wack names. It's like, pick a struggle already. If I was you, I would just challenge him to a freestyle battle. That would make him stop bugging you. You could beat him in your sleep."

Rahim thought Kasia was the smartest person he knew, but sometimes it seemed like she understood how computers worked better than she understood how people did. Her parents homeschooled her (although sometimes Rahim thought she was schooling them). She didn't understand the rules of the middle school jungle. Demarcus rolled with an entirely different set of kids. He and Rahim might as well be from different planets. Demarcus was from Planet Cool Kids and Rahim was . . . not. Embarrassing Man Man again would just make things worse.

"You know what really made him mad was that comment Gaia2K left on his song. 'Lazy, lackadaisical lyrics that are linguistically lugubrious. That's a lot of *L*s, and Man Man deserves all of them.'" Kasia collapsed into a torrent of giggles.

Rahim sat down on the floor. Iago flew over and landed on his shoulder. Iago's little stubby metal-segmented legs gripped his T-shirt.

"Gaia2K is a fan of Four the Hard Way too. She isn't down with all that mumbling," Rahim said. "When did you give him legs?"

"I didn't. I installed internal upgrade software into his central processing unit. Now he can do his own upgrades if he feels like he needs to." Kasia rolled her stool over to a dresser that sat in the corner. She rooted around inside one of the drawers. "How do you know Gaia2K is a girl? That could just be a screen name."

"I guess you got a point. I just kinda assumed."

She rolled over to where Rahim was sitting, clearing her throat. Iago flew back to Kasia's desk. She held a small rectangular package, encased in gaudy holiday wrapping paper.

"What is this?"

"Your birthday present," Kasia said.

"My birthday isn't until June."

"Time is an arbitrary concept. Open it."

Rahim shrugged and ripped open the paper. "Is this . . . a phone? You didn't have to buy me a phone."

Kasia frowned. "I didn't buy it. I built it. Plus, I know how bad you wanna watch those old Four the Hard Way videos on YouTube. I don't get why you like them so much."

"Um, because they're the best rap group in history?"

"Yeah, that broke up in 2000 and haven't made a record since. I don't even know how you got into them."

"I told you, when I went down to my uncle Shaka's in Virginia last summer. He played their music for me every single day. Too Smooth, Rock G, MC Juice, and the Sultan are lyrical geniuses. Their wordplay is amazing, the beats are phenomenal, and you can actually understand what they are talking about. Like the way they play off each other, how their styles come together. It just . . ." Rahim trailed off.

"I mean, I know you like them, but I gotta tell you they sound kind of goofy. I can make beats better than theirs by accident."

"You take that back!" Rahim said, but he was smiling. He knew Kasia was just teasing. No one really understood his fascination with a band that broke up twenty years ago. Not his best friend, not his parents, and least of all Man Man, who seemed to take pleasure in insulting Four the Hard Way every chance he got. Rahim sometimes wondered why Man Man hated them so much, but he realized guys like that didn't need a good reason to hate anything. Demarcus probably hated ice cream for being too cold.

"Anyway, I fixed it so it uses satellite signals through a ghost router. So you won't have to pay a phone bill. It also has a kinetic battery. The phone charges when you shake it," Kasia said.

Rahim turned the phone over in his hands. It had an electric-blue plastic casing and a glass touchscreen. There was a green LED at the top of the rectangle of glass and a red one at the bottom. "Is that legal?" he asked.

"What?"

"The satellite thing."

Kasia stared at him for a long time before finally saying, "Yeah. Sure. As long as the light is green, you're fully charged. When the red light comes on, you only got two minutes of juice left. Now you can do your homework at home."

"How am I gonna come over here to record if I'm doing my homework at home?"

"I don't know. Tell your parents the truth. You wanna be a famous rapper."

"It sounds stupid when you say it like that," Rahim said.

"It's only stupid if you think it is," Kasia said. "You wanna lay another one down before you go?"

"Nah, I better get back. Thank you. I guess I gotta get you something now," he said.

"I told you, time is just a social construct," Kasia said.

"You know that's weird, right?"

"If you really want to get me something, there is an astronomy exhibit coming to the Franklin Institute next month."

"You want tickets to a museum?"

"I could hack the system and get them myself, but you're the one saying you gotta repay me."

Rahim stood and held up his hand. Kasia gave him a high five. "Thanks for this. I mean it."

"No biggie. Let me know how it works."

"Hey, this isn't gonna be like those X-ray glasses, is it?" Rahim asked.

"Nah. It's better!"

Rahim wasn't sure he liked the sound of that.

Rahim slipped in the back door and headed for his room, passing his mom on the stairs.

"You get what you needed?" she asked.

"Yeah, I got it."

"Did you memorize it?" she asked.

"What?" Rahim stopped.

His mother turned and smiled at him.

"You didn't take any notes," she said.

"I—I . . . uh . . . ," Rahim stammered.

"It's okay. There's nothing wrong with wanting to see your friends." She disappeared into the living room.

Kasia's smart, but she ain't smarter than my mom, Rahim thought.

2

THE NEXT MORNING, AS he and his sister headed to school, Rahim had a feeling this was going to be a good day. Well, as good as a day spent avoiding Man Man trying to give him an atomic wedgie could possibly be. He couldn't wait to show his new phone to Harris. Now maybe everyone else would stop looking at him like he had two heads because he didn't have a cell phone.

He could dream, couldn't he?

Harris was putting his coat in his locker when Rahim turned the corner. Their lockers were side by side, which was how they'd become friends. That and their mutual outsider status. Harris was taller than Rahim but slim with shoulder-length dreads.

"I never knew you could run so fast. You could make the Olympics if you had Demarcus chasing you all the time," Harris said.

"Ha-ha. So funny." Rahim put his backpack and his coat in his locker. Then he reached into his back pocket and pulled out the phone. "Hey, check this out," he said.

Harris stared at him. "What is it?"

"It's a phone, duh."

Harris didn't say anything for almost a full minute. Then he burst out laughing. "Dude, that looks like a brick somebody threw at you or something."

Rahim felt his face get hot. "Kasia made it for me."

"I'd make her take it back," Harris said.

"Why are you saying that? I can get videos on here and everything on it."

"Do you have to wind it up? What is it, like, an iPhone version negative one?" Harris said, laughing again.

"You know what, man, forget it. It was a cool thing for her to do."

"No, it wasn't," Harris said, catching his breath. "Man, why don't your folks just get you a phone? I know your dad's kind of strict when it comes to computers and stuff, but, like, a phone is like . . . what's that word when you gotta have something?"

"A necessity," Rahim said.

"Yeah. If I was you, I'd give that back to Kasia and get a phone that don't weigh fifty pounds. Well, maybe there is one good thing about it."

"What's that?" Rahim asked, knowing Harris was

going to make another joke but just wanting to get it over with.

"If Man Man chases you today, you can throw it at him."

Later in English class when Mr. Kyoto showed them a movie about a neighborhood bodega, Rahim almost had the phone confiscated.

"Mr. Reynolds, I need your attention on the screen, not your phone. This film is a great lesson about story-telling. Also, I'm in it along with another famous Phila-delphian. We were both child actors at the time," Mr. Kyoto said.

"'Another'?" Harris whispered. Rahim had to put his head down to keep from laughing.

In math class, Dayna Givens asked him if she could see it.

"Sure," Rahim said.

Dayna was the smartest person in class and the best player on the girls' JV basketball team. She was nice to the outcasts like him and Harris, but was down with the cool kids like Man Man too. (Rahim didn't really think Man Man was cool. Everyone was just too afraid of him to tell him that.)

"Wow. Did this belong to one of your parents? I've never seen a phone this old. Is it, like, a family heirloom?"

Rahim sighed. She wasn't making fun of him. She actually thought he had a hand-me-down phone. It would have almost been better if she had made fun of him.

By the time Man Man slammed him against his locker at the end of the day, he was hoping he'd knock the phone out of his hand so he wouldn't have to keep it. He didn't want to hurt Kasia's feelings, but her gift had lowered his social standing. Rahim didn't think that was possible, but here he was. He was just taking the phone out of his locker when Demarcus and his sidekicks rolled up on him.

"Yo, why you walking around with that suitcase?" Man Man asked.

"It's just something my friend gave me," Rahim said. Man Man pushed him against his locker again.

"Yo, for real, your phone's as wack as your lyrics," Man Man said. "Punk. I don't even feel like giving you the reverse atomic wedgie." His two sidekicks snickered. "Then again, you still look like you think you got more swag than me." He spun Rahim around and grabbed the waistband of his underwear.

"Demarcus, I know I don't see you grabbing a fellow student," Mr. Rutkowski said. Everyone froze. Mr. Rutkowski was the physical education teacher and the basketball coach. He was also over six and a half feet tall. No one mouthed off to Mr. Rutkowski.

Man Man let go of Rahim. "Nah, son."

"What did you say?" Mr. Rutkowski asked. He crossed his massive arms.

"No, sir," Man Man said in a low voice.

"Why don't you three come with me? Rahim, go on home." Mr. Rutkowski herded Man Man and his sidekicks down the hall. Rahim shoved his phone in his pocket and grabbed his coat.

"I should've just dropped it," he said to himself.

When he got home, Rahim saw a note from his mother and father saying they were out getting groceries. He slammed the door and stomped up to his room. Harris was right. Even if his dad thought having easy access to a computer was going to rot his brain, that didn't mean he couldn't at least let Rahim have a decent phone. He would never understand why his dad seemed to hate technology so much. Maybe he'd had a bad experience with a calculator as a kid.

Rahim closed the door to his room and fell across his bed. Horror movie posters fought for space with old-school hip-hop posters on his walls. N.E.R.D., Bone Thugs-N-Harmony, Outkast, and his Four the Hard Way posters took up the most space. Two bookshelves full of horror novels and a few mysteries lined the far wall. Other than those few possessions, his room was sparse.

Rahim pulled the cell phone out of his back pocket and touched the screen. It lit up with a pale greenish light. His name was in Old English letters across the top of the screen. There were also several icons for different apps. Rahim tapped on the search engine icon. Yesterday he'd told an eensy-weensy lie about having a social studies paper due. Today his teacher actually assigned them a paper. Might as well get a start on it. He typed the words *Philadelphia Public Library* into the search bar. His paper was about the library system—one of his favorite subjects. The phone might be a hideous blue, but he could still use it to do his homework. He just wouldn't take it to school again. Ever.

The screen glowed as the green LED on the top blinked on and off like it was winking at him.

"Don't tell me this gonna die already." Rahim shook the phone up and down with both hands.

The screen began to glow brighter.

"Come on."

The screen flickered in time with the green LED.

I should've asked her how long I gotta shake this thing, he thought.

The screen stopped flickering and went black. Rahim stopped shaking the phone.

"Did I break it?"

In a flash the screen glowed so bright it hurt his eyes. He squeezed them tight. At the same time, a strange sensation flowed over his whole body. It was like he was swimming in warm, gooey water.

The white light from the phone died down.

He no longer felt like he was swimming. He felt cold. No, scratch that—he was *freezing*.

Rahim opened his eyes.

"What the . . . ?" he said, but his words trailed off into a muffled grumbling. He suddenly realized why he was cold.

He wasn't in his room. He was standing on the sidewalk in front of the West Side branch of the Philadelphia Library. Rahim shook his head. People filed around him as his mouth gaped open.

"I gotta be dreaming," he said to no one in particular. He almost pinched himself, but he knew for a fact he wasn't dreaming. The cold stinging his cheeks told him that much.

"Oh man. Oh man. OH MAN." He wasn't sure how far the library was from his house, but he was sure he hadn't sleepwalked over here.

"Man, it's soooo cold," Rahim said.

"You got that right." Nodding, a homeless man pushed a shopping cart past him. Rahim stared at the back of the man's head as he continued down the street. He could have sworn he'd seen him before.

Rahim touched the screen on his phone. Maybe this was some computer simulation Kasia had installed in the phone. No, that was silly. He wasn't even wearing a VR visor. He had to get back home. He could figure it all out once he got out of the cold. He touched the screen and pulled up the map icon. He didn't know if he had enough for a cab and he wasn't sure if there was a subway nearby. He typed in his address and hit ENTER.

The green LED began to flicker on and off again.

"Oh, come—" Rahim began to say.

The phone glowed with the same blinding white light.

"—on," he finished.

Rahim looked around. He was standing in front of his house.

"What is going on!?"

It didn't matter. Right now, it was too cold to be standing outside without a jacket. Rahim went in the house and closed the door behind him.

"I didn't hear you leave," his dad said, sitting in his chair, but this time he had a larger book in his lap. Rahim stopped short.

"I thought you and Mom were at the grocery store," Rahim mumbled.

"We've been back for an hour. I thought you were upstairs doing your homework." Dad closed his book.

"Um . . . I, uh . . . went out the back door. I went over to Kasia's earlier, and I thought I had dropped something."

"What?"

"Huh?"

"What did you think you had dropped?" Dad asked. He folded his hands in his lap and stared at Rahim.

"Uh . . . my notes from class today," Rahim said. He headed for the stairs.

"How's the homework coming?" his dad asked.

"Almost done," he said over his shoulder.

Once he was back in his room and sitting on his bed, he hit the phone icon. He knew Kasia's number by heart, but she had programmed it into the phone.

"You coming over to do another track?" Kasia said when she answered.

"What's wrong with this phone?" Rahim said. His fingertips were still numb.

"Well, since we're talking on it, I'm gonna say nothing," Kasia said.

"For real, what's wrong with it? I did a search for the library website and the next thing I know I'm standing in front of it. Then I put in my address and poof! I was back here. Tell me what's wrong with this phone," Rahim said.

"Okay, calm down. First of all, are you sure that's what happened? Like you didn't fall asleep and dream that you were at the library?" Kasia asked.

"I didn't fall asleep. I'm telling you this phone is, like, magic or something," Rahim said.

"Magic is just science we don't understand. I still think you fell asleep. I mean, I'm good, but I'm not that good."

"I'm bringing it back. I'll be right there."

"Now hold on. Let's do a little experiment. Do a search for my address. No, I tell you what, do a search for a place you've always wanted to go. Let's see what happens."

"Uh, nope. I'm just bringing this thing back," Rahim said.

"Look, you're telling me I accidentally invented a teleporter. I think you're having a hallucination."

"This ain't a hallucination, Kasia! When I typed in the address for the library, my parents were out getting food. I come back to the house, and they say they been home for an hour. This is X-ray glasses all over again," Rahim said.

"Okay, just calm down. I mean, on the one hand, you might really have teleported. But on the other hand, if you are . . . making a mistake, we can figure it out. And if you're right, what's the worst that happens?"

Rahim pulled the phone from his ear and peered at it. Was it possible he had imagined the whole thing? If he was imagining it and he ended up at Kasia's, that wouldn't be that bad, would it?

"Hold on."

Rahim typed in the place he wanted to go to more than any other. A place he had dreamed about going. A place that was literally impossible for him to go to unless Kasia's phone was a teleporter and a time machine.

The green light began to flicker as the screen began to glow.

"What's happening?" Kasia asked.

"The green light is blinking and the screen is glowing," Rahim said.

"Uh-oh."

"What do you mean 'uh-oh'? Kasia, what is uh-oh?"

"It means the power source I used might be a . . . little bit unstable."

"What should I do?" Rahim yelled.

Before Kasia could answer, the swimming sensation overwhelmed him as bright white light filled his field of vision. The world around him seemed to fade away in bits and pieces as he began to float into that white light.

3

"RAHIM!" KASIA YELLED INTO her mic. "Rahim, are you all right?"

"I . . . I don't know."

As the light from the phone receded, Rahim became aware of several things all at once. One, he was hot. He was wearing a long-sleeved fleece hoodie over a black T-shirt, and he could feel himself starting to sweat through both of them. Two, he was *not* in his room. Three, well, three was the most unbelievable part of all.

"Are you at home?" Kasia asked.

"No. I am definitely not at home." Rahim took a step back and raised his head. He was standing in front of an old-timey-looking box office. Above the entrance was a marquee. Rahim took another step back.

"Oh man. Oh man," he warbled.

The marquee was advertising tomorrow night's show.

"Where are you? What did you type in the search bar?" Kasia demanded.

"I was just fooling around. I didn't think it would

really work. I was starting to think you were right and I had just imagined everything."

"Where are you?"

"I always wanted to see Four the Hard Way in concert," Rahim said.

"Rahim, they broke up before we were alive. How were you gonna see them in . . . Uh-oh," Kasia said.

"I hate it when you say uh-oh," he said.

"You searched for their last concert in 2000, didn't you?"

"No. Worse. I typed in 'Four the Hard Way first show in Philadelphia.'" Rahim heard Kasia's fingers fly over her keyboard.

"Rahim, that was in June 1997."

"No duh," he said.

"Are you sure that's where you are?" she asked.

"I'm standing right in front of the place. Their name is on the sign. The show is tomorrow night. Everyone is wearing FUBU and Cross Colours. FUBU, Kasia. That's what my uncle is wearing in all his old high school pictures." He paused. "Kasia, I would like to come back home now," Rahim said. Sweat trickled into his eyes, stinging them.

"Okay, I guess I tapped into something stronger than a regular communications satellite. All right, we can fix this. I can fix this. Is the green light on?"

"Yes," Rahim said. Cars rolled by him blasting songs by Jay-Z, Wu-Tang, Das EFX. All the great classics of hip-hop were rumbling from radios that pushed enough bass to make his chest hurt. A Jeep drove by playing Biggie Smalls.

Biggie never got to perform with Four the Hard Way, Rahim thought. A quiet sadness joined the terrifying fear slowly taking over his mind.

"Okay, um . . . if you really are in the past, all you need to do is type in your address and the year and you should just come back home," Kasia said.

"Are you sure?"

"Yeah. Pretty sure."

"O-o-kay," Rahim said. He typed in his home address and the year and pressed SEND. The green light began to flicker. The screen began to glow.

Then it winked like a candle caught in the wind. The red light began to blink weakly.

"The red light came on. Should I shake it?" Rahim said.

"I think it's more than that," Kasia said softly.

"What do you mean? You built this thing. What's wrong with it?"

"Nothing's wrong with it. But—"

"No, no buts," Rahim said. Two kids about his age walked by him. They were both sporting flattops and wearing classic Jordans.

They're not classics yet, Rahim thought. He could hear Kasia typing furiously.

"Okay, so I used three satellites that technically belong to the US government so you wouldn't have to pay a bill. I thought I was just breaking into some high-level government network, but it looks like it was way more than that."

"Kasia, I would very much like to go home now," Rahim said.

"It appears one of them was some sort of temporal flexibility generator. The other one must be a subatomic teleportation initializer."

"English, Kasia. English."

"One is a time-fluctuation facilitator and the other one is a quantum-transportation device."

Rahim didn't respond.

"One takes you into the past; the other one moves you from place to place within the current timeline," Kasia said.

"Okay, so why isn't it working?" Rahim asked.

"It looks like they may have locked us out of the system."

"WHAT?"

"Don't freak out. I can hack it again. It's just gonna take me a little while. Might have to route it through a system in Beijing."

"All right, well, when can I come home?" Rahim asked.

"I don't know just yet, but I'll get you back."

"I knew I shouldn't have took this phone," Rahim moaned.

"Hey, I was trying to do something nice for you," Kasia said.

"You sent me back in time!"

"Technically, you sent yourself back in time."

"Kasia . . . ," Rahim said.

"I'm working on it right now."

As Kasia pounded the keys, the doorbell rang. She ignored it and kept attacking the new and improved firewall that had been installed on the communication satellite's system. Or, more accurately, the system that controlled the time-fluctuation facilitator. Kasia pushed a curl out of her face. When she had first found the secret government network, she'd just been playing around. Getting into the system had been more of an accident than anything else. Now she was trying to get into the network on purpose.

That was a little bit scary.

"Kasia, can you come downstairs, please?" her mom hollered from the ground floor.

"Kinda busy, Mom," Kasia yelled back.

"That wasn't a request, young lady," came an unfamiliar deep, rumbling voice. Kasia froze. She got up from her stool and crept over to the staircase. Standing at the bottom step were two huge men in identical gray suits and black sunglasses. Kasia went back to her computer.

"Rahim, I gotta go."

"Go? Go where? What are you talking about? You have to get me HOME," Rahim said.

"I know, but I think the people who own the satellite are here. Look, I'll handle things on this end. You make sure you get somewhere safe, and whatever you do, don't interact with anyone. The smallest change in past events could have terrible consequences."

"How am I supposed to not interact with anyone?"

"Just stay away from people."

"I'm on the street. It's nothing *but* people!"

"Young lady, we need to speak with you. Now," came a different deep, rumbling voice.

"I gotta go, Rahim. I'll be right back." Kasia hit the ESC key and all her monitors and computers completely shut down.

Rahim stared at the phone. The line had gone dead. He turned in a lazy circle.

"This can't be happening," he said.

"Oh, it's happening all right," said a homeless man in a Hawaiian shirt pushing his shopping cart. A brother pulling what appeared to be a stand-up bass in a black nylon storage bag sidestepped the homeless man. The bag had the initials C.M. embroidered on the back.

Rahim looked at the phone one more time before shoving it in the pocket of his jeans. This was so much worse than the X-ray glasses.

There was a part of him that didn't believe any of this was real. Maybe Kasia had been right. Maybe he was stretched out across his bed, drooling on his pillow. Yeah, maybe that was what was happening.

Except . . .

Everything felt so real. The cars driving that looked brand-new but also incredibly dated to him. The people walking by in ridiculously out-of-date clothing. Rahim was never going to be called the most stylish kid in the seventh grade, but even he knew baggy jeans and oversize white T-shirts were not in style. One kid passed with pants that were so baggy, Rahim thought if a breeze caught him just right, they would puff up like a parachute and take him away.

Kasia had said for him to stay away from people, but that was impossible. Kasia was smart. She was the smartest person he knew, but staying away from people in the middle of the summer in Philly was like trying to dive in a pool and not get wet.

Maybe if I just walk around and don't talk to anybody. That should be good, Rahim thought. He took off his fleece pullover and tied it around his waist. That helped a little, but he was still sweating through his shirt. He started walking down the street, doing his best not to bump into anyone. There was a little voice in the back of his head whispering that this was all a dream. That in reality he was safe at home in his bed waiting on his mother or father to knock on his door and wake him up for dinner.

Every step he took made that seem less and less likely. He passed a newsstand. He stopped, turned around, and grabbed a magazine off the rack.

"Don't pick it up if you ain't gonna buy it," the man running the newsstand said. Rahim put it back, but not before noting the date and the year. June 1997. He wasn't asleep. He wasn't dreaming. This was really happening. Rahim felt the bottom fall out of his stomach. He started walking again. He took quick steps as he wandered the streets. If Kasia couldn't get this stupid phone fixed, what was he going to do? How would he find something to eat? Would he have to sleep on the street?

He turned left at the corner and kept walking. Street vendors were hawking portraits of Allen Iverson on velvet, Sixers and Eagles jerseys, watches, heavy gold chains, and pagers.

"Hey, my man, you want that new Bahamadia joint? How about Philly's finest!" a man yelled at Rahim.

Rahim stopped and looked at the man's stand. He had dozens of small plastic squares lined up on top of a table covered with a red velvet cloth. Each plastic square was covered in artwork and photos.

"CDs! You selling CDs!" Rahim said. Most of the kids in his class didn't know what CDs were. A lot of them had never even seen one in real life. But Rahim had studied all the cover art for Four the Hard Way's three studio albums and their three mixtapes. He didn't own any CDs, but he knew what they were.

"Yeah, I got you, son. What you looking for?" the man asked. Before he knew it, Rahim was talking to the vendor. He knew what Kasia had said, but she had to be exaggerating a little bit.

"You got any Four the Hard Way?" Rahim asked. The man flipped through his CDs and pulled out one with a black-and-white photo of the four members on the cover. It was a simple picture that was at odds with their larger-than-life personalities. Just the four of them standing under a streetlamp.

"Wow, this a classic," Rahim said.

"Well, I don't know about that. It just came out last week," the vendor said.

Rahim blinked. "Oh yeah. It's not a classic . . . yet," he said. He put the CD back on the table. Even if he bought it and got it home, he didn't have a way to play it.

"You know this new kid DJ Drama? He just dropped a Native Tongues mixtape."

"Nah, I'm good," Rahim said. He kept walking down the street. He knew the performance venue wasn't that far from his house. Or where his house would be in the future. Maybe he should head over to his neighborhood and see if someone could help him. He didn't really have a logical reason why he thought this, but this wasn't a logical situation. If he was being honest, he really just wanted to see some familiar surroundings.

He crossed the street and headed for home. Or what was going to eventually be his home.

After cutting through some alleyways and across some busy streets with more potholes than he remembered, he took a right turn and found himself one street away from home. A deep sense of sadness fell over him like a heavy coat. Nothing here looked familiar at all. Mr. Daniels's corner store was a video store. Mrs. Rollins's used bookstore was a flower shop. He didn't even see Mr. Carlson's sandwich shop.

Rahim sat down on the sidewalk in front of the flower shop. He didn't seem to have the energy to take another step. He was in trouble. More trouble than he had ever been in in his whole life. He was lost in his own city in a time and a place that he didn't understand at all. He felt hot stinging tears well up in the corner of his eyes. He rubbed at them with the back of his hand and took a long, deep breath.

"Hey, you okay?"

Rahim raised his head and saw a girl about his own age standing over him. She had long braids that hung down her back.

"Yeah, I'm okay. I'm . . . I'm kinda lost, that's all," Rahim said.

"You wanna come in and use our phone? Call somebody?" the girl asked.

"Nah. I'm good. I got turned around. That's all. There was a bookstore here once, but I guess that was a different time," Rahim said.

"That's creepy," the girl said.

"Why you say that?"

"Well, because I'd like to open a bookstore one day. I told my dad when he retires I'm gonna turn the flower shop into a bookshop. We'll sell used and rare books by Black authors and we'll sell doughnuts. He hates when

I say that," the girl said with a smile. Rahim looked at her. Really looked at her. If you gave her a touch of gray in her braids and added a couple of inches to her height, she'd be the spitting image of Mrs. Rollins.

"Of course. It's 1997," Rahim mumbled.

"All year," the girl that would one day be Mrs. Rollins said.

"I guess I should get going."

"You sure you don't want to come in and use the phone?"

"No, thank you. I need to get somewhere and think."

"You know, when I want to think, I go to the library. It's quiet. No one bothers you, and they have air-conditioning."

"That's actually a good idea. Yeah, I'll go hang out at the library until this all gets straight. Thanks," Rahim said. He got up off the sidewalk and brushed the dirt off his pants. He was halfway down the street when the girl yelled to him.

"Hey, what's your name?"

"Ra—Ronald. My name is Ronald," Rahim said. He thought about what Kasia had said. It probably wasn't a good idea to tell Mrs. Rollins his real name.

"See you around, Ronald," she said. Rahim waved at her and crossed the street.

Twenty minutes later, he was standing at the base of the steps to one of the larger branches of the Philadelphia Library. Rahim thought the building looked like a castle that someone had dropped in the middle of the city. As he started up the steps, he heard a voice that froze him in place.

"Reynolds, didn't I tell you to have my money or a new pair of sneakers next time I saw you?"

Rahim held his breath. Whether he was dreaming or actually in the past, he couldn't seem to escape Man Man. He closed his eyes and prepared himself for the headlock that he knew was on its way. That was when another voice piped up.

"I've told you I don't have any money and I don't wear sneakers!"

Rahim turned to his right. He saw three bigger kids surrounding a smaller kid wearing glasses and a short-sleeve shirt and necktie. The kid in the necktie was trying to balance a tall stack of books as the bigger kids pushed and shoved him.

Who wore a necktie in the middle of summer if they didn't have to?

"I don't care about that, cornball. That's not my problem. I told you next time I see you and you didn't

have my money or my sneakers, I was gonna fold you up and put you in a mailbox," the biggest kid said. He and his two friends were wearing baggy jean shorts and oversized Phillies baseball jerseys and high-top sneakers. Each of them had on a backward snap-brim baseball hat. They took turns pushing and shoving the kid in the tie. The kid was trying to hold his own, but Rahim could see the fear building in his eyes. This wasn't the first time he'd been pushed around, and it wasn't going to be the last. Rahim knew that feeling.

"Hey," Rahim said. The word was out of his mouth before he realized what he was doing.

The three bigger kids stopped bouncing the kid in the tie around like a soccer ball and turned to face him. The skinniest guy said, "Tyrone, check out this dude."

"Oh no," Rahim whispered.

"You say something, punk?" Tyrone asked as he and his two sidekicks turned to Rahim. Rahim took a step backward and readied himself to run.

"Me? I didn't say nothing. I just had something in my throat," Rahim said. He took another step backward.

"You about to have my fist in your face," Tyrone said.

A girl who looked a few years older than Rahim and the kid in the necktie appeared from around the corner. "Come on, y'all. Leave them alone, Ty." She was about the same age as the bullies.

"This ain't none of your business, Tisha."

"Okay. I guess I'll just go and page Shaka. See how he likes hearing about you picking on his little brother," Tisha said. The three boys stepped away from the kid in the glasses and necktie.

"Ain't nobody scared of your boyfriend," Tyrone said. Still, he and his buddies gave the kid in the glasses a final hard shove, knocking his books to the ground, and headed off.

"What you looking at?" Tyrone said. He bumped his shoulder into Rahim as he walked past him. Rahim felt like someone had thrown a brick into his chest.

Rahim didn't recognize the girl. But he recognized the name Shaka. His uncle was named Shaka. And if Shaka was this kid's brother, that meant he was—

"Dad?" Rahim said with a gasp.

4

"KASIA SIERRA!"

Kasia knew her mom was serious when she used her first and middle names. She adjusted her glasses as she headed down the stairs.

"Iago, go into stealth mode," she said.

When she reached the bottom of the staircase, her mom was standing there holding one of her clay sculptures. Kasia could never tell when her mom's sculptures were actually done. She just waited until her mom put them on the mantel and asked Kasia and her dad what they thought. Her dad was wearing his favorite apron and holding a wooden spoon as he stood next to her mom. He gave Kasia a quizzical look, then turned his attention to the front door.

The two men in the gray suits were standing just inside the doorway, no longer wearing their sunglasses. Both of them had their hands behind their backs and had similar features. Faces like a cinder block with a mouth drawn on it in a thin, flat line.

"Kasia, these gentlemen said they need to speak with you about something to do with a satellite?" her mom said.

"Uh-oh," Kasia whispered.

"Hold on now. What is this about a satellite?" her dad said. He pointed the spoon at the agents like it was a sword.

"Your daughter is a very smart young lady," one of the men said.

"A little too smart," the other man said.

Her mom and dad looked at each other.

"What agency did you say you were from again?" her mom asked.

"You guys with the CIA? FBI? NSA?" her dad asked.

"Yes," they responded in unison.

"I—I don't think I'm going to let you talk to our daughter until we speak with our lawyer," her dad said.

One of the men reached inside his suit pocket.

Kasia watched as her dad pulled her mom back and shook the wooden spoon at the two walking refrigerators. "Hey, let me see your hands!" he shouted, but then stopped, looked at the spoon, and lowered it sheepishly.

"It's not a gun, Dad. There's no outline in his coat," Kasia said. Everyone stared at her for a long time. She shrugged her shoulders and sat on the step.

"Let me introduce myself. I am Agent Brown. My

associate is Agent Green. This is a warrant for the seizure of all her computer equipment, signed by the US secretary of defense. We are here to execute the warrant."

"Now, just hold on one minute. What exactly are you accusing my little girl of?" her dad said. He was a slim man, but Kasia thought he looked like he had doubled in size. She could tell he was mad.

"Your *little* girl hacked into three Level Omega satellites that are the property of NASA in conjunction with the United States military," Agent Green said.

"What?!" her mother exclaimed.

"They were pretty easy to get into," Kasia admitted.

"Kasia, please," her dad said.

"Those satellites were designed by two Nobel Prize winners!" Agent Brown said.

"I hope they didn't get their prize in cybersecurity," Kasia said.

"Kasia, hush," her dad said. He bit his bottom lip as he scanned the warrant. Finally, he raised his head and zeroed in on the agents. "You can execute your warrant, but we're not saying another word without a lawyer."

The two agents looked at each other, then started up the stairs. Kasia didn't move. Agent Green tried to step over her but couldn't get his leg up high enough. He changed his mind and shimmied past her. His partner followed suit.

"How'd they know where her computers were?" Mom asked.

"They're with the government. They probably know what toothpaste we like," Dad said. He squatted in front of Kasia so they were eye to eye. "Just what were you getting into, Button?"

Her dad had light brown eyes that seemed to sparkle when he laughed or when he was concerned. They were sparkling now as he gently stroked his goatee.

Kasia bit her bottom lip just like her dad.

"I was just trying to—" Kasia stopped herself. It suddenly dawned on her that if Rahim was stuck in 1997, he wouldn't be home for dinner. If she told her parents the truth, they might not believe her, but they would believe she knew where Rahim had gone. She couldn't get tied up in a neighborhood search. She had to figure out how to get him home. Getting stuck hanging up missing-person posters would just slow her down.

"—do some research about the Philadelphia Experiment and thought those satellites might have something to do with it," Kasia finished. Her dad cocked his head and looked at her.

"Is that the truth, Button?" he asked.

"I was just messing around online, looking into teleportation and stuff like that," Kasia said. Technically, that wasn't a lie. Well, not a big one.

"Okay." He stood.

The agents came downstairs carrying her external hard drives, computer, and monitors.

"Could you get the door for us, sir or madam?" Agent Green asked. Dad sucked at his teeth before opening the front door.

"You'll be hearing from our lawyer," he said.

The agents nodded as if they heard that a lot.

As they walked past, Dad cleared his throat. "You guys think she found out about your Philadelphia Experiment?"

"That experiment never happened," Agent Brown said.

Agent Green stopped in front of Kasia's dad. "But if it did and we thought she had hacked into those files, we'd be offering her a job." He nodded at Kasia, retrieved a card from his pocket, and handed it to her dad. Then he followed his partner out the door.

"Well, that's not how I pictured the evening ending," Mom said.

"I'm gonna call Dontae. See if he can make sense of this warrant," Dad said. "If we get your stuff back, no more hacking satellites, young lady."

Kasia went back upstairs to her workspace-bedroom. She sat in her desk chair and touched the temple of her glasses.

"Iago, come out of stealth mode."

Above her head a gentle whirring started. As the seconds passed, the soft white, feather-brushed surface of her ceiling began to shimmer like waves of heat coming off a hot stove. When the shimmering stopped, Iago detached from the ceiling and landed on her now-empty workspace. Her desk looked so strange without her equipment on it. They'd taken nearly all her stuff.

Kasia sighed. She'd broken into the Philadelphia Experiment files last year. It had never occurred to her that the government might be continuing those experiments with satellites instead of high-intensity magnets. She supposed it made sense, though. Even though the original experiment in World War II had been a failure, the data they'd acquired was invaluable. Kasia had gotten interested in it after watching a documentary with her parents. According to the documentary, the Philadelphia Experiment was either a huge urban legend or the United States Navy's attempt at trying to harness invisibility for their battleships. If the documentary was to believed, instead of invisibility, the scientists had stumbled upon teleportation and perhaps even time travel.

Kasia sat in her chair and put her feet up on her desk. She'd read the top-secret files the government had kept about the experiment. She was pretty sure it wasn't an urban legend. The scientists must have taken the information they had discovered that night in October and used it to create the satellites she'd had the bad luck to hack.

"All right, Iago. Let's get my stuff back. I can't leave Rahim stuck in the past. Him just being there is probably already messing up the timeline." Kasia leaned forward and put her thumb on the corner of her desk. An infrared scan read her thumbprint. A few seconds later, a hidden drawer in her desk opened silently. Kasia reached inside and pulled out the tablet that contained her notes on Iago. She had a feeling that one day Iago and his AI software were going to be important. She knew that hacking was risky, so she didn't keep any of the drone's information on her main computers or in the cloud, in case a day like today came to pass. If it wasn't for Rahim, she'd let them keep her setup and would build a new one, but she didn't have time for that. Rahim needed her help now, and those agents had the only tools that could bring him home.

She got up, opened her window, and touched the temple of her glasses again. The right lens suddenly gave her Iago's perspective of the room. With a tap on the tablet, a map of the city popped up. She touched it again and a red dot appeared on the map.

Kasia had installed tracking software on all her computer equipment. Because even though they lived in a decent neighborhood, there wasn't any sense in taking chances.

"Iago. Go," Kasia said.

Iago flew out the window, banked hard to the left, and disappeared into the horizon. Kasia pulled on her jacket and slipped out of her room and down the stairs.

"Mom, Dad, can I go to the library? I mean, since those guys took all my stuff," Kasia asked. Her dad was still on the phone with her uncle Dontae. Her mom came into the living room.

"I think that's okay, honey. Be back before dark. And don't worry. We are gonna get this sorted out, okay?" she said. Her mom kissed her on the forehead. Kasia returned the gesture.

"Oh, I know we will," Kasia said before heading out the door.

5

"WHAT DID YOU SAY?" his dad asked.

Well, the kid standing in front of him wasn't really his dad. Not yet. Rahim shook his head. This was all getting so confusing.

"Huh?" Rahim said.

"I said, what did you say?" Omar asked. He readjusted his tie. Tisha started to pick up the books that lay scattered on the sidewalk.

"Uh . . . I said dang." Before Omar could respond, Rahim bent down and helped Tisha pick up the rest of the books. One of the books was called *NEATE to the Rescue!* Rahim handed it to Tisha, who put it on top of the pile and then handed the whole stack to Omar.

"So, you don't just read history books?" Rahim asked. Tisha and Omar stared at him.

"How'd you know he reads history books? I ain't never seen you before," Tisha said.

"Um . . . I . . . uh, was in the library, and I saw him in the history section."

"I didn't see you in there," Omar said.

"I was hanging out in the back," Rahim said.

"The back?" Tisha asked.

"Yeah, way, way back."

Tisha eyed him warily, then shrugged.

"Anyway, Omar, your mom wants you to come home for dinner. She said if somebody didn't come get you, you'd spend the night here."

"Where's Shaka at?" Omar asked.

"He's helping your dad at the shop. They had an emergency call, so when they left, I decided to go home. The library's on my way, so I told your mom I'd look for you," Tisha said. "You better get going. It'll be dark soon."

Rahim looked over the city's skyline at the setting sun. She was right. He wondered if he could hide out in the library. He'd read a book once about some kids who lived in a museum for a while.

"Okay, okay, I'm going. Thanks for coming to get me."

Omar held out his hand toward Rahim. "Thank you too."

Rahim shook his hand.

"I didn't do nothing but say hey."

"You didn't pretend like nothing was happening. So, thanks."

"What's your name, anyway?" Tisha asked.

"Ronald." Rahim remembered what Kasia said about timelines and changing history.

"Well, Ronald, you better get home too," Tisha said.

Rahim looked down at his shoes. Suddenly he felt incredibly sad. He did want to go home. He missed his room. His mom. His sister. His dad—even though the kid standing in front of him was his dad, as crazy as that sounded.

"You okay?" Tisha asked.

"I can't go home," he said, and his voice began to crack. He didn't want to cry again, but he felt like his tears had a mind of their own.

"Hey, hey, what's wrong? Why can't you go home?" Tisha asked, her huge hoop earrings jingling as she cocked her head and stared at him.

"I just can't, okay." Rahim's face suddenly felt hot.

"You know, maybe you could come to my house. My parents can help you figure out how to get home," Omar said.

"Omar, you don't know this boy. You can't just invite him to your house," Tisha said. "No offense, Ronald."

"It's okay. I'll figure something out." Rahim took a deep breath.

"He tried to help me. I can try to help him. Like you said, it's getting dark."

Tisha threw up her hands. "Your mama's gonna flip

her lid if you bring this boy home. But you gonna do it, ain't ya? All right, well, I'm going home. I did my part. See ya later." And with that, Tisha headed up the street.

"Is she right? Are you going to get in trouble if I come to your house?" Rahim said.

"Maybe, but my mom and pop always tell me to do what's right even if it's hard. Especially if it's hard. Come on. Maybe they'll let you stay for dinner. She's making oxtails tonight."

"Thanks, Da—d-d-dang it," Rahim said.

"Here, you can take some of these books for me. I always end up getting more than I can carry."

Just like when we go to the bookstore, Rahim thought.

"My house isn't that far away."

"I really appreciate this, man."

"Don't worry about it. My mom and pop will help you out. They always talking about how we gotta look out for each other. They let my cousin Ellis stay with us last summer when his parents broke up. I'm pretty sure they won't mind. So, you just move to Philly? I don't remember seeing you around."

Before Rahim was forced to come up with another lie, his phone began to ring.

6

KASIA SQUINTED AS SHE peered through the right lens of her glasses. Iago was flying high above the city. He zipped over Independence Hall, banked hard to the right, then flew past the Philadelphia Museum of Art. Kasia checked her tablet. According to her map, the agents' car had stopped at the corner of Ludlow and 30th Street next to a fancy coffee store that Kasia heard her parents talk about sometimes.

As she made her way down the sidewalk, she alternated between studying the map and focusing on Iago's bird's-eye view of the city and the agents' vehicle. Kasia side-stepped a woman pushing a double-decker baby carriage and touched the temple of her glasses. Iago's camera increased its magnification. She could see that the agents had pulled over and stopped in front of a hot-dog stand.

Kasia checked her map. She was less than two blocks from that hot-dog stand. She was 90 percent sure Iago could handle what she had planned, but she wanted to be as close as possible in case it was too much for her robotic best friend. Rahim was her human best friend.

Really, he was her only human friend.

Kasia hurried down the street and cut through an empty lot. She emerged near a bus shelter. She touched her glasses again and watched as the two agents got out the car and took their place behind two older ladies standing at the hot-dog cart. Kasia noticed they hadn't locked the car.

Kasia sat on the bench inside the shelter. She pulled her knees up to her chin and rested the tablet there as she pulled her coat tighter around her shoulders. She would never understand why some people said they loved the winter. Or the summer. She was a fan of spring and fall. Her mom told her that was a good way to look at the world.

"It's called moderation, Button," her mom had said one day.

"Iago, go into stealth and descend sixty feet," Kasia said. The drone descended quickly before coming to a stop twenty feet above the vehicle.

"Iago, go under the car and deactivate the battery," Kasia said. Almost immediately she was given a whirling, spinning view of the street and the car as Iago flew under it and up into the engine.

"Ain't that that weird girl who works at the vegan store? Is she talking to herself?"

Kasia looked up and saw six kids around her age standing near the bus shelter. Three girls and three boys. One of the girls had on a thick, puffy black Pittsburgh Penguins ski jacket, and her long, luxuriant hair was braided into thick locs. One of the boys was wearing a black wool coat and a winter cap with the words MAN MAN. Another girl had on a thick red flannel shirt with matching red earmuffs. The third girl was sporting a comfy-looking hoodie with a picture of the Little Mermaid emblazoned on the front. The two other boys had

on nearly identical jackets and hats. She recognized most of them but couldn't recall their names. She was fairly sure they came into her parents' store with their parents from time to time. She'd heard Rahim talk about Man Man, but she'd never met him. Until now.

Man Man answered his own question.

"Yeah, you're that girl. Why don't you go to school? Is something wrong with you?"

Kasia ignored him and continued to study her tablet.

"Is she, like . . . like, can she talk?" one of the other boys asked.

"Look at her shoes. What are *those*!?" Man Man said.

Kasia straightened her glasses and rolled her eyes.

"Nothing you say bothers me because I don't care what you think. I don't know the rest of you, but you can get a better friend than Man Man, who keeps trying to be a rapper but writes lyrics like he is trying to audition for *Sesame Street*. Now, if you don't mind, I'm busy," Kasia said.

"Dang, Demarcus!" the girl in the earmuffs said.

"My name is Man Man. It's on my hat!" Man Man said. He took a step toward Kasia.

"You take one more step and I'll use the Taser on my tablet to give you a two-thousand-volt attitude adjustment," she said. Kasia didn't have a Taser built into her tablet, but she knew Man Man wouldn't know that. He already thought she was weird. Might as well take advantage of it.

"Whatever. That's why you sitting here by yourself catching the bus," Man Man said.

"Rather be alone than be friends with you," Kasia said.

"Whatever," Man Man said again before heading down the street followed by his crew.

Kasia shook her head slowly. Was that what Rahim had to go through every day? No wonder he was so uptight.

"Okay, back to it. Where is the battery? That's not it.

What is that? Is that the AC?" Kasia said as she guided Iago through the car's undercarriage.

"Hotness," she said as Iago's camera settled on the battery cables.

Through the drone's audio, she heard a deep voice boom: "I can't believe he ran out of hot dogs. How do you run a hot-dog stand and run out of hot dogs?"

"I'm feeling hangry," another voice said. Kasia heard two car doors slam.

"Oh snap! Hurry, Iago. Get that cable."

She saw the cable rapidly approaching Iago's camera as the little drone crawled over the motor.

"What in the world does 'hangry' mean?" the first voice asked.

"Hungry and angry," the second voice said.

Kasia saw Iago's tiny gray metal limbs grip the cable.

"You wanna get some Mexican food?" the first voice asked.

"Cut it. Cut it now, Iago. Come on, little guy." Kasia tried not to think about what would happen to Iago if the engine started.

"Now! Cut now!" Kasia yelled. She saw the tiny metal pincers squeeze into the heavy rubber coating of the battery cable.

Agent Brown turned the key in the ignition just as the pincers cut through the cable. The engine started to turn over, but died before any of the various belts and pulleys had a chance to crush Iago into little pieces. Kasia let out a deep breath.

"That was close, Iago. All right, let's wait until they get out and call somebody to pick up the car. It's too cold for them to stand on the street for long," Kasia said with a shiver. The temperature had dropped a couple of degrees since she had sat down on the bench.

When the car was on a tow truck, it would be easier to get her stuff back. A disabled battery would do the trick.

Kasia heard the doors to the car open, then slam. She heard the muffled phone conversation of one of the agents through the microphone she had installed in Iago that was connected to the Bluetooth speaker in the temple of her glasses. They were talking about the "check engine" light and debating the possibility that someone had forgotten to put oil in the car.

Twenty minutes later, their car was being loaded onto the back of a tow truck. At least she thought it was being loaded on a tow truck. Iago was still in the engine.

"Okay, where you want me to take this jawn?" a voice said.

"Six hundred Arch Street," Agent Green said.

"Dang, that's the FB—"

"We know what it is," the agent said. There was silence for a few seconds.

"All right, then," the tow truck driver said.

"Don't stop for anything. We'll be right behind you," Agent Brown said.

"If we can get someone to come get us," Agent Green mumbled.

"Got it," the tow truck driver said. Kasia heard him get into his truck and slam the door. A moment later, the car shuddered as the truck eased into traffic.

"Okay, Iago, go now." Kasia touched the temple on the right side of her glasses, and Iago slipped out of the engine. She studied her map again. The tow truck was riding down Market Street. It'd be getting off soon if it was heading to Arch.

Iago climbed over the car and headed for the trunk. Seeing through his eyes, Kasia used one of his pincers to force the lock and open the trunk. The tow truck driver didn't seem to notice.

"Oh, my babies." All Kasia's stuff was in a neat pile.

"Iago, tie the power cords together." Working quickly like a metal-and-plastic gnome, Iago wove all the power cords together like a long braided piece of rope.

"Okay. Let's dip, Iago. Full power," Kasia said.

Iago's propellers whizzed to life as his metal legs gripped the power cords and ascended out of the trunk and straight up into the overcast winter sky. Most drones could barely lift ten pounds, but Kasia had designed Iago with engines and appendages that were four times as strong as a regular drone. She'd done it for the same reason she did a lot of things. To see if she could.

Kasia scanned the horizon for a few moments until she saw Iago flying over the city with her equipment. She tapped the tablet to make sure its GPS was set to her address. Then she exited the bus shelter and headed home. The agents would definitely notice she had reclaimed her stuff, but that was another problem for another day. The most important thing was getting Rahim back safe and sound before something she couldn't fix happened.

If it hadn't already.

7

"IS THAT A REMOTE control?" Omar asked. "Why are you carrying a remote control in your pocket?"

Rahim was holding the phone and staring at the screen. It had vibrated so hard he thought it was getting ready to explode. The number that came up on the screen was not Kasia's. It wasn't any number that he knew. It was actually a mix of numbers and letters and a few strange symbols that didn't make any sense to him.

"Did you swipe your parents' remote?" Omar asked. Rahim looked at his dad. No, he had to start thinking of him as Omar. His day was already weird enough without calling a kid his own age "Dad."

"No, it's a phone," Rahim said.

Omar laughed. "Oh man, that thing is the size of a brick. I bet you don't get no service," he said.

"You'd be surprised," Rahim said. The phone had not stopped ringing. There was something so strange about the numbers and symbols on the screen he was almost afraid to answer the call.

"Well, you gonna answer it or what?" Omar said. Rahim looked at the phone again. If it was Kasia, maybe she was calling to tell him she had a way to get him home. He answered the phone.

"Hello?"

"Okay, I'm working on breaking back into the satellite network. But you gotta make sure you interact with as few people as possible," Kasia said.

Rahim looked at his dad, er, Omar. "Uh-huh," Rahim said.

"Is that your parents?" Omar asked.

"Ra, where are you? And who are you with?" Kasia asked.

"It don't matter. When can you get me home?"

"Um, I'm no expert in time travel or teleportation, but I'm learning fast. You being in the past will change things. The longer you're there and the more people you get involved with, the more things are gonna change. I read a book on time-travel paradoxes about twenty minutes ago," Kasia said. "This can get really bad. Now, you wanna tell me who you're with?"

"No. Call me when everything is fixed," Rahim said. He hit END before Kasia could say another word. He hated hanging up on her, but his head was beginning to hurt from thinking about what she was saying. Plus, he didn't want her to know he'd done the one thing she'd told him not to do.

She just needs to concentrate on getting me home, Rahim thought.

"Was that your people?" Omar asked.

"I'm almost positive it wasn't," Rahim said. Omar gave him a quizzical look, then shrugged his shoulders.

"Let's get going. I been up here all day, and I'm pretty hungry," Omar said.

"You sure your, uh, parents won't mind me coming over?" Rahim said. He almost said "my grandparents" but caught himself. Omar scratched his head.

"My mom is pretty cool. My pop is too except he's on it about school. Like he doesn't mind me coming to the library and hanging out all day, but he'd flip if I went to the basketball courts or something."

"He's pretty tight on you, huh?" Rahim asked.

"You have no idea. He already has a college picked out for me when I graduate high school. Same with my brother, Shaka," Omar said.

"That kid that was picking on you, what's his deal?" Rahim asked.

"He's just got it in for me because he blames me for him flunking fifth grade last year."

"How is that your fault?"

"Because I wouldn't let him cheat off my paper," Omar said.

"That makes no sense at all," Rahim said.

"It's Tyrone. It don't have to make sense. All summer he been picking on me like it's my fault his mother made him go to summer school. I usually can avoid him or hope my brother's around. They get real quiet when I'm with Shaka," Omar said.

"He looks out for you, huh? Shaka, I mean," Rahim said. He thought of his uncle and his wide frame and big hands.

"Well, kinda. I mean, he don't let those fools do anything to me, but sometimes he acts like he don't want me around. I guess that's how big brothers are. But he's mostly all right. It seems like I don't see him as much during the summer. He's either helping my pops, hanging with Tisha, or playing basketball," Omar said.

"You like basketball?" Rahim asked, pretty sure he already knew the answer.

"Duh," Omar said.

"Huh. What's your favorite team?" Rahim asked. The idea his father had liked sports as a kid was news to Rahim. Back home, his father barely acknowledged sports was a thing.

"The Sixers. Who else would it be? Why? Who's your favorite team?"

"Oh, Sixers definitely. I was just asking."

"Too bad they ain't make it to the finals. You think the Bulls gonna beat the Jazz?" Omar asked. Rahim didn't need a smartphone to tell him the Bulls had beaten the Jazz. Anyone who liked basketball knew that fact.

"I'm pretty sure they will."

"I don't know. I mean, I like Jordan and all, but I think the Mailman got him this year. My uncle Cy said he bet the farm on the finals. My mom says that means he wasted a lot of money on it," Omar said.

"Who is Uncle Cy?" Rahim asked. This name was new to him.

"My pop's brother. He's staying with us for a while. I think he broke up with his girlfriend," Omar said.

They walked past a record store. The sign above the door said it was DEMARCO'S RECORDS, CDS & TAPES. Rahim had never seen a vinyl record or a cassette tape, but through the front door, DeMarco's selection of CDs looked like an ocean. It made the street vendor's selection look like a drop in a bucket. There was a poster in the window advertising an upcoming show.

"You don't like Four the Hard Way, do you?" Rahim asked. If his dad liked sports as a kid, maybe his dad liked hip-hop too. His dad. He was walking and talking with his dad. And his dad was . . . kinda cool? Rahim didn't know what was more shocking—the fact he had traveled back in time or that his dad was once actually pretty fun to be around.

"No, I don't like them," Omar said.

"Oh," Rahim said. He wasn't shocked, just a little bit disappointed.

"I don't like 'em. I LOVE THEM. They are my favorite group. It's them, Wu-Tang, and Black Moon." Omar then started rapping one of Four the Hard Way's first hits, "Black Knight."

> We the last of a dying breed
> Got more than you think up our sleeves
> Bring more heat than ATL in the summer
> You can call us rappers like you call Mario a plumber
> Technically correct but missing the point
> We the ones the gods have come to anoint
> This the one time you should believe the hype
> My lyrics cut like Excalibur so call me the Black Knight

By the time they crossed the street, they were both rapping in unison. Around another corner, Omar stopped in front of a two-story house with a black gate.

"This is our place. Like I said, my mom is cool but my pop can be kinda funny. Hey, don't talk about Four the Hard Way. My pops isn't a fan."

Rahim didn't recognize the house. In the present, his

grandparents lived in Alabama. They'd sold the house before he was born.

"Yeah, my dad ain't a fan either," Rahim said.

Omar opened the gate, and they walked up to the front door.

"Hey, Mom, I'm back!" Omar yelled as he entered the house. Rahim stood on the step with his hands in his front pockets. The phone was in his right hip pocket. Kasia's warning popped into his head again. Rahim had the feeling if he stepped through the door, he was crossing some kind of line. One that couldn't be uncrossed.

"Boy, why you yelling? Lord have mercy, I ain't deaf," his mom said. She appeared in the doorway with her hands on her hips. She was tall and slender with a cropped haircut. She was wearing a dark blue uniform. A name tag on the left side of her blazer said LOTTIE. A patch on the right side said SEPTA.

"Sorry, I thought you were still in the kitchen," Omar said.

Lottie nodded, then studied Rahim. "Dinner's been done. Also made rice and beans. Got some iced tea in there too. Don't eat it all. Your daddy and your brother will be back in a few. Don't let your uncle eat it all neither. Who's your friend here, O?" Lottie asked.

"This is Ronald. He's lost," Omar said.

Lottie glanced at Omar, then turned her gaze back on

Rahim. Rahim, for his part, couldn't stop staring. The person he knew as his grandmother was a sweet, stooped woman with a head full of gray curls who slipped him twenty dollars when they visited Muscle Shoals. The woman standing in front of him was a world away from Nana L. The woman standing in front of him now looked like she could smell a lie from a mile away, and when she did, you wanted to be two miles away from her.

"Is that right, Ronald? You lost?"

"Uh, yes, ma'am," Rahim said.

"Uh-huh. You sure you didn't get mad because your mama told you to clean your room and you decided to run away?"

Rahim swallowed hard. "No, ma'am."

Lottie sighed. "Well, what's your parents' phone number?"

Rahim scuffed his toe against the concrete steps. He knew both his parents' cell phone numbers, but what good would it do to call them? If he wasn't having a dream (and he was positive it wasn't a dream at this point), they were thirty or so years in the future. He wasn't a tech genius like Kasia, but he was pretty sure a regular phone wouldn't be able to connect that call. And if he gave his grandmother his phone and she was somehow able to get through to his parents, well, then what? They couldn't help. They'd probably just jump on Kasia and ask her a million questions, which would slow her down as she tried to get him home.

No, he was on his own. At least until he heard from Kasia again. He took a deep breath. Rahim rattled off a number but quickly said, "It might be cut off." He was getting really good at lying.

Lottie studied him even harder. "Well, come on inside and we'll give it a try anyway. You hungry?" she asked.

In fact, he was hungry. He was actually starving. Did time travel make you hungry? He'd have to ask Kasia.

"Thank you, ma'am," Rahim said.

"You can call me Ms. Lottie if you want."

"Thank you, Ms. Lottie," Rahim said.

"Can I call you Ms. Lottie?" Omar asked.

"Not if you want to keep living in this house." His mom tapped him playfully on the head as she ushered them inside. The house was small but cozy. The scents coming from the kitchen made Rahim's stomach growl. On the way to the kitchen, Rahim saw a slim man sitting on a couch in the living room watching a basketball game on the television. Rahim guessed the guy was Omar's uncle. He looked up as the three of them passed by.

"Hey, Uncle Cy," Omar said.

"Hey, bighead. Who's this?" Cy pointed at Rahim.

"This is Ronald. He's lost," Omar said.

Rahim started to say hello when out of nowhere his

vision became blurry. No, that wasn't exactly right. It was more like the whole room was wrapped in shimmering, transparent gauze. Rahim saw it move over him like a wave crashing into the beach and then it was gone. Rahim stumbled before catching himself.

"Are you okay, Ronald?" Ms. Lottie asked.

"Did you see that?" Rahim asked.

"See what? That's just my uncle Cy," Omar said.

"Do you feel all right, Ronald?" Ms. Lottie asked with noticeable concern.

Rahim shook his head. "I'm fine. I just tripped."

"Let's get you some water," Lottie said as she led the boys to the kitchen.

"Welcome, folks, to the beginning of our coverage for the 1997 NBA finals between the Houston Rockets and the Detroit Pistons," a voice from the television said.

Rahim started to say something, but he told himself he hadn't heard the announcer correctly. It was 1997 and everyone knew it was the Bulls and the Jazz in the NBA Finals. He'd just misunderstood what the announcer had said, that was all.

That had to be it . . . right?

Rahim shook his head and continued after Omar and Ms. Lottie into the kitchen.

8

KASIA FOLLOWED IAGO ALL the way home until he flew through her open bedroom window. When she got upstairs, she saw that Iago had deposited all her equipment on her bed. After about fifteen minutes, she had everything hooked up again with a few slight modifications.

She installed a new, stronger firewall that would hide her systems from any prying eyes. She then set up a program to bounce her IP address all around the world every five seconds. Then she ran downstairs, got a bowl of her dad's vegetarian chili, and brought it up to her room.

I'm no good at hacking on an empty stomach, she thought. Back in her chair, she started trying to break into the government satellites again between spoonfuls of shredded jackfruit. Her dad said jackfruit was a healthy vegetarian alternative to meat, so he used it in his chili. Kasia thought it looked like a giant walnut with weird, soft, pulpy skin. Rahim said it tasted like soggy cardboard, but Kasia liked it, especially with her dad's secret sauce.

She was halfway through the first satellite's security system when there was a knock at her door. Kasia jumped up and opened the door a crack. Her mom was standing on the landing with a worried frown on her face.

"Hey, Mom," Kasia said cautiously.

"How was the library?" her mom asked.

"It was okay," Kasia said.

"Kasia, Mrs. Reynolds just called."

"Uh-huh?" Kasia knew what was coming next.

"She's looking for Rahim. He isn't in his room, and he's not at the library. I told her he wasn't here. She can't find him anywhere."

Kasia gulped.

"He didn't say anything to you about sneaking out, did he?"

"No, he didn't say anything to me." Technically, that was true. Rahim definitely had not said anything about going back in time to her before he did it.

"Kasia, you're telling me the truth, right? This is very serious." Her mom's frown deepened. Kasia knew this was her mom's super-serious face.

"No, Mom. He didn't say anything to me about going anywhere," Kasia said.

"Okay. Your father is still on the phone with your

uncle. He's trying to see if he will cut his vacation short to help get your laptops back."

"Aw, Mom. It's not a big deal. I don't want Uncle Dontae to come back early from Australia for me."

Her mom took a deep breath and stepped into the room. Kasia could hear her sigh.

"Kasia, you may not think it's a big deal, but it's important that we stand up for ourselves. Now, those men may have had a warrant, but that doesn't mean them coming in here and taking your things was right. Your uncle is one of the very best attorneys in the country, and he will gladly get on that twenty-three-hour flight to help his only niece."

Kasia snuck a quick glance over her shoulder. "Really, Mom, it's okay. Trust me," Kasia said. Her mother smiled at her, but it wasn't her usual full-face dimple-cheeked smile. Usually when her mom smiled, it lit up her whole face and made her light brown eyes sparkle. But this time her smile vanished almost as fast as it had appeared.

"Don't worry, we gonna get this straightened out. And if Rahim comes by here, please let me know so I can let his mom know, okay? It's important."

"I will, Mom."

"That's my girl." Her mom turned and walked back down the stairs. Kasia returned to her desk and let out a deep sigh. She couldn't help but feel a little guilty. Dr. and Mrs. Reynolds were probably worried sick about Rahim. If she was being honest, she was getting worried about him too.

"All right, let's get you home, homie." Kasia's fingers flew over the keyboard. First things first. She had to ease his parents' minds about him being missing in action. She pulled up the file that had all the songs they had recorded together. She used her sound-editing program to pull snippets of Rahim's voice out of the songs. Then she searched for the Reynoldses' home phone number. She knew that they had one of the last landlines in all of Philadelphia.

The phone rang once before his father's deep voice answered. "Hello. Rahim, is that you?"

Kasia pushed ENTER on her keyboard.

"It's me . . . I'm . . . fine. I'm at . . . the library to learn . . . some skills." The program sounded like Rahim if he was impersonating a robot.

"What? Let me tell you something, son. You have exactly ten minutes to get back and explain to me and your mother why you left the house without telling anyone where you were going," Dr. Reynolds said. Kasia didn't have to see his face to realize he was on the verge of being very angry.

"No problem . . . I'll be there . . . lickety-split, leave you leaning like the Tower of Pisa with more hits than Goku or Frieza."

"Oh snap!" Kasia quickly pushed some buttons on her keyboard.

"What . . . what did you just say to me?" Dr. Reynolds said.

"Gotta go," the simulation said.

Kasia ended the call. "Yikes. I hope by the time I bring you back your dad has chilled out."

Kasia then called Rahim. She wasn't sure how the phone signal was able to cross time and space, but she had an idea. She'd read an article on a science website about quantum computers and how the quantum dynamics could be used for communication in the future. Kasia had a feeling the government had solved that problem and the future was now.

Rahim took forever to answer the phone.

"Ra, where are you? And who are you with?" Kasia asked.

"It don't matter. When can you get me home?"

"Um, I'm no expert in time travel or teleportation, but I'm learning fast. You being in the past will change things. The longer you're there and the more people you get involved with, the more things are gonna change. I read a book on time-travel paradoxes about twenty minutes ago," Kasia said. "This can get really bad. Now, you wanna tell me who you're with?"

"No. Call me when everything is fixed," Rahim said.

The line went dead.

He.

Had.

Hung.

Up.

On.

Her.

"Oh, you are so lucky you're my friend or I'd leave you right where you are," Kasia said out loud to herself as her hands flew over her keyboard.

9

RAHIM FINISHED HIS LAST spoonful of beans and used a napkin to wipe his mouth. Omar had loosened his tie while he ate his dinner. He finished off his glass of juice with an exaggerated *ahhh.*

"Boy, you so silly," Ms. Lottie said. As she gathered up their plates and washed them in the sink, Rahim heard the front door open, then close with a loud slam. An older man walked into the kitchen followed by a tall kid with a high-top fade. The man was dressed in dirty blue khakis and a gray work shirt. The name SAM was stenciled over the left front pocket of the shirt. On the right pocket the words SAM'S HANDYMAN SERVICE were embroidered in blue thread on a white background.

"You get it fixed?" Ms. Lottie asked.

Mr. Reynolds grunted and gave her a kiss on the cheek. "Yeah. I told Gus he gotta stop letting his people pour hot grease down the only working drain in his restaurant. Then, while we were there, his freezer went on the fritz, so we had to fix that too."

Rahim tried not to stare at Mr. Reynolds. The grandfather he knew bore little resemblance to this man with the broad bowling-ball shoulders and wide hands. The grandpa Sam he knew was a kindly old man who liked to play solitaire on the front porch in his sweatpants. This Sam was tall with muscles that strained against the sleeves of his shirt.

"You save me anything to eat, Booger?" the kid with the high-top fade said as he put Omar in a playful headlock.

"Let me go," Omar said with a hint of a laugh.

Although forty pounds lighter and four inches shorter, his uncle Shaka was easy for Rahim to recognize.

"Who's this?" Grandpa Sam asked as he jerked a thumb toward Rahim.

Ms. Lottie dried the last plate and put it in the cabinet. "This is Ronald. He's a friend of Omar's. He says he's lost and it's no use calling his parents because his phone is off. I tried to call and nobody answered," Mrs. Reynolds said. She and Sam exchanged a quick glance.

"Is that right, son?" he asked.

"Yes . . . yes, sir," Rahim said. Sam smoothed down his shirt.

"Yo, why your jeans so skinny, dog?" Shaka said, laughing. "Look like you wearing tights."

"Shaka, hush," his father said. He crossed his arms and leaned against the sink. "There's nobody you can call, son?"

Rahim shook his head. Mr. Reynolds sighed.

"You better call Johnny Law, Sam. That boy might be on a milk carton," Cy yelled from the living room. His grandfather rolled his eyes.

"You think that's what we should do?" Ms. Lottie asked.

"I'm not calling the cops on a Black kid who's lost. Or a runaway," Mr. Reynolds said. He looked at Rahim when he said this. They locked eyes for the briefest of moments before Rahim dropped his head. He was definitely lost. There was no doubt about that at all.

"Can he hang out with us for a while, Pops?" Omar asked.

"You really don't know any other way to get in touch with your parents? I know they gotta be worried about you if they don't know where you are."

You have no idea, Rahim thought. "No, sir," he said.

Sam let out a breath. "Let's do this. You can spend the night, then tomorrow we go down to the social service building and see if they can help you."

"Come on. I'll show you my room!" Omar said.

"Before you show him your room, show me your book report," Sam said.

"You gotta do book reports during the summer?" Rahim asked Omar.

The whole house got quiet.

"My boys are both gonna be college graduates. They both have to do book reports and math assignments when they're out from school. While the rest of these kids running the streets, my boys are getting ahead of the game," Grandpa Sam said.

"Every game should have a time-out," Shaka murmured.

"You got something to say, Shaka?"

"Nope, Pop."

"Go get your book report and then you can show him your room," he said. Omar got up from the table and went over to the pile of books he and Rahim had carried from the library.

"Do you know your home address?" Ms. Lottie asked Rahim.

"Two twenty-four St. Albans Street," Rahim said. "But my parents aren't there." Technically, that was the truth.

Grandpa Sam sighed again. "Where are they, then?" he asked.

"They are far, far away," Rahim said.

Ms. Lottie clucked her tongue.

Omar walked back into the kitchen and handed his father a piece of paper.

"*The Rockpile* by James Baldwin. Nice one. Glad to see you made good use of your time at the library."

"Can I show Ronald my room now?" Omar asked.

"Yeah, but, Ronald, after he shows you his room, we are gonna take a ride over to your house. Just to make sure your parents are far, far away," Grandpa Sam said.

Rahim swallowed hard. "Yes, sir."

"Come on," Omar said. Rahim followed Omar through the short hall and up a narrow staircase to the second story of the house. There were two doors to their right and one to their left. At the end of the hall up another flight of stairs was an attic door. Omar opened the second door.

"This my room. Shaka moved his room to the attic. Said he needed his privacy. That's fine by me."

Just as Rahim was about to follow Omar into his room, he saw something flickering out the corner of his eye. He turned his head to the right and saw a figure standing at the end of the hall by the attic door. The figure was wearing some type of helmet that covered their entire face like a fencing mask, a long metallic-green trench coat, a black vest, and a white shirt with a red silky scarf around their neck.

Rahim stopped. "Hey, is that another uncle?" he asked.

"Who?" Omar asked.

Rahim nodded his head to the right. "Whoever this is here in the hall."

Omar poked his head out the door. "What are you talking about?"

Rahim turned back to the figure, but it was gone. "Huh?" he said.

"I think the heat done boiled your brains." Omar laughed.

Rahim didn't join in the laughter. He knew there had been someone standing in the hallway. He hadn't imagined it. As he was trying to decide just how crazy he might be going, his phone rang.

"YES!" RAHIM SAID. He pressed the green button on the screen as he stepped back into the hall. "Please tell me you fixed it?"

"First, don't hang up on me again. That's rude," Kasia said. "Second, let me guess: You didn't stay away from people like I told you to, did you?"

"What? How do you know . . . Why would you say that?" Rahim asked.

Kasia groaned. "I checked my homework while I was getting back online with the satellite. Of the three different systems, the communications one is the easiest and—"

"Wait, you were checking your homework while you were breaking into a satellite?" Rahim said.

"Duh, you know I'm a multitasker. Anyway, I was reading my history homework and there are things in the file I don't remember or I remember differently. It's fascinating, actually."

"What? I don't understand," Rahim said.

"Listen. I do my homework on the same computer I used to design your phone. It uses the same network as the satellite, which is the same network your phone uses, which is basically a quantum computer. Theoretically, it's on the same temporal wave as your phone."

"Uh-huh," Rahim said. He didn't understand anything she was saying.

Kasia kept going. "The phone and my computer are still on the old timeline. You know, the one that existed before you did what I told you not to do. Since the information in those files is stored in a quantum cloud, it's not affected by the changing timeline. Think of it like this: It's like we wrote a message and put it in a bottle. Then we threw it in the ocean. No matter what happens in the ocean, what we wrote on that message ain't gonna change," Kasia said.

Rahim didn't say anything.

"Look, that's the best way I can explain it right now."

He closed his eyes. "Do me a favor. Use your other computer—the one that's not on the network, the one we use to record—and check something for me," Rahim said.

"What do you want me to check?"

"Who won the 1997 NBA championship." He heard the click and clack of computer keys.

"The Detroit Pistons beat the Houston Rockets, four–zip," Kasia said.

"Aww, man," Rahim said.

"I guess that's not what you remember?"

"My uncle is a big basketball fan. He talks about the Chicago Bulls' dynasty all the time," Rahim said.

"Yikes. Okay, obviously your being there is changing things. Right now, it's just a basketball game. But it could get worse. Don't talk to anybody else. Go somewhere quiet and just stay there until I can break into the other two satellites and get you home," Kasia said.

"You got any suggestions where I should go? It's a hundred degrees here, and I don't have any money."

"I don't know. Let me think for a minute," Kasia said. "Wait, where are you right now?"

Rahim didn't respond.

"Ra? Where are you?"

Rahim looked over his shoulder. His dad . . . er, Omar was pretending not to listen to his conversation. He was playing with the rook from a chessboard as he sat on his bed.

"I'm at Omar Reynolds's house," Rahim said.

"Who?"

"Omar Reynolds. You know, he's Rahim's father."

Kasia was quiet for a moment, and then she let out a long groan.

"You're unbelievable. That's the last place you should be and the last person you should be around. You've already changed the timeline and cost the Bulls a championship. You could do something that keeps your parents from meeting and having you and your sister. You ever heard of the butterfly effect?" Kasia yelled.

"Look, I didn't have a lot of places I could go."

"Oh boy. When you mess up, you go for the gold," Kasia said.

"Hey, you're the one who gave me this phone," Rahim said.

"Oh, excuse me for trying to be nice to my friend."

Rahim closed his eyes. "Look, I'm sorry, okay? I'm kinda scared, K."

"I know, Ra. Just . . . I don't know. Try not to do anything to draw attention to yourself. The less you interact with people, the less likely it is you'll change the timeline any more than it's already changed. Meanwhile, I'm gonna get back to work on the other two firewalls."

"Okay. Hey, have my parents noticed I'm not there yet?" Rahim asked.

"Oh, I took care of that," Kasia said.

"How?"

"Trust me, I got you on that. You just stay quiet and out of the way."

"Okay. Hey, who's the president?" Rahim asked.

"William Edwards. Who was it when you left?" Kasia asked.

Rahim let out a sigh. "Don't worry about it."

"Remember, stay out of the way. I'll call back again when I'm done."

"All right," Rahim said. The phone went dead.

"Was that your parents?" Omar asked as Rahim walked into the room.

"Nah."

"Can I ask you something?" Omar said.

"Sure."

"Did you parents, like, abandon you?"

Rahim didn't know how to answer that. He was really tired of lying. "I don't want to talk about it. Show me your room," he said.

Omar got off the bed and went to a small wooden desk in the corner. He grabbed an action figure. "I've got almost all the *Dragon Ball Z* figures. This is Goku," he said.

"You're into anime?" Rahim asked.

"Mainly just *Dragon Ball*. My pops doesn't let us watch too much TV. But my brother has a DVD player in his room and he lets me use it sometimes." Omar put the figure down and pulled a book from a shelf above the desk. A spiral notebook tumbled out.

"This is where I keep my comic books. My pop doesn't like them, but I think they're cool." Omar opened the book and showed Rahim that it was actually a box. There were several issues of the *X-Men* comic in the box.

"What's that?" Rahim said, pointing at the spiral notebook. It had a black cover. The words *The Cypher* were written on the cover with a white grease pen.

"Um . . . promise you won't laugh."

"I mean, I'll try not to laugh. I can't make no promises," Rahim said.

"For real. Promise," Omar said.

"Okay, I promise."

"It's my rhyme book."

"You write your own rhymes? I can't believe it!"

"Why? You don't think I could spit any lyrics?" Omar sounded hurt.

"No, it's not that I don't think you could do it. It's just surprising, that's all."

"They're not that great, but it's kinda fun to write my own stuff."

"Why are you hiding it? Does your dad hate music too?" Rahim asked.

"I don't think he hates music. He just doesn't want anything to take our minds off of school," Omar said.

"Yeah, he's on it about school," Rahim said.

"I guess it's because he didn't get to graduate. He had to go to work. He tells me all the time how he wants us to do better."

"I get that, but doing book reports during the summer? I got a friend that's homeschooled, and even she gets the summer off. Your dad is intense," Rahim said.

"You have to be intense if you're going to succeed," Grandpa Sam said, appearing in the doorway.

Rahim and Omar jumped. Omar closed the box he was holding and put it back on his shelf.

"Come on, Ronald. I'm taking you home."

"Can I go too, Pop?" Omar asked.

"No. You stay here and get started on those math problems I gave you yesterday," he said. "Let's go, Ronald." Omar shrugged, and Rahim gave him a nod in return.

"See ya," Omar said.

"Yeah, see ya," Rahim said. His grandfather had already started down the stairs. As Rahim left the room, he gave the far end of the hall a wary glance, then headed down the stairs.

Rahim climbed into the passenger seat of the work truck. Grandpa Sam started the engine, and they slipped into the westbound traffic. Rahim pulled out the phone. The red light was slowly pulsating while the green light was still dark.

"Your parents must care about you an awful lot if they got you that fancy phone, don't you agree?"

Rahim stared out the window. The sun had set, and the city had come alive in a way it only did during the summer. Rahim was hit with another wave of homesickness. This was his city, but this wasn't his home. Not this Philly, not in this time.

"I asked you a question, son."

Rahim bit his lip. Kasia could be a tad sarcastic if you didn't know her, but she was also one of the smartest people he knew. Who else could accidentally build a teleporting time machine? If she said he shouldn't talk, he wouldn't talk. So, Rahim just shrugged his shoulders.

"Okay. You don't wanna talk. I get it. But when someone asks you a question, you owe them a response. That's called respect," Grandpa Sam said.

"I'm sorry. My friend got me this phone, not my parents." Rahim grimaced. What if those eleven words made an asteroid hit the earth in the future?

"I still think your parents probably care about you a lot."

"I know," Rahim said. He glanced out the passenger-side window. He didn't want to think about how terrified his parents would be when they realized he was missing. They could be strict sometimes and his dad seemed to have a grudge against technology, but he never doubted that they loved him.

Grandpa Sam took a left turn, then a right. About twenty minutes later, they turned onto St. Albans Street and looked out the window, studying the building numbers.

"Two twenty, two twenty-two . . . Well, I'll be," Grandpa Sam said. The building at 224 St. Albans Street had once been a two-story structure. But now it was a burned-out husk covered in soot. He double-parked and let the truck idle.

"You really don't have anywhere, else to go, do you?" he asked.

Rahim shook his head. He didn't know what he expected to see at his future address, but a burned-out building was not on the list.

Grandpa Sam pinched the bridge of his nose. "All right, you can spend the night, but tomorrow we are gonna figure out how to find your people."

"Okay, thank you, sir," Rahim said.

I'm already with my people, he thought.

They headed back to the house. Omar and Cy and Shaka were in the living room, watching the final minutes of the game.

"The Rockets got this," Shaka said.

"I hope not. I got fifty bucks on the Pistons," Cy said. He tapped his left foot as the minutes on the game clock ticked away.

"The Pistons win this game," Rahim said as they entered the house. They all turned their heads and looked at him. While they were staring at him, the announcer on the TV started yelling into his microphone breathlessly.

"The Pistons win with a last-minute three-point shot. The Pistons win!"

Cy leaned his head back and laughed long and hard. "Boy, you hit that one on the head. You wanna pick the rest of the series for me?"

Without thinking, Rahim said, "The Pistons sweep the Rockets."

"Shucks, you sound so sure, I'll put the rest of my paycheck on that!" Cy said.

Rahim squeezed his eyes shut. He needed to fill his mouth with a big wad of bubble gum.

Not talking was easier said than done.

11

DR. AND MRS. REYNOLDS SAT in the living room staring at their front door. Dr. Reynolds checked his pocket watch. It was almost eight o'clock. Rahim had called them at five saying he was on his way home. Dr. Reynolds put the watch back in the pocket of his vest.

"Don't yell at him when he comes home," Mrs. Reynolds said.

"I won't yell. But I will speak in an elevated tone so as to impress upon him the folly of his actions," Dr. Reynolds said.

"Honey, that's yelling," Mrs. Reynolds said. Dr. Reynolds didn't respond. Mrs. Reynolds drummed her fingers on her knee. She was about to suggest they go look for Rahim when she heard the back door slam. She exchanged a brief glance with Dr. Reynolds before they jumped up and ran to the kitchen. They had expected to see Rahim, but the kitchen was empty. As they stood there bathed by the harsh LED lights in the ceiling, they heard a door slam upstairs. Dr. Reynolds headed up the stairs, taking them two at a time.

Dr. Reynolds banged on Rahim's bedroom door. "Rahim, open this door!" The tone of his voice was quite elevated.

"Sorry, Dad. I feel . . . sick. I need to . . . sleep," came the reply. The voice sounded muffled through the door.

"Boy, if you don't open this door—" Dr. Reynolds said.

Loud snoring sounds rumbled their way from the other side of the door. Dr. Reynolds turned to his wife.

"I'm going to get the keys, then Rahim and I are going to have a discussion."

Mrs. Reynolds shook her head.

"What?" he said.

"Rahim is entering a new stage in his life. He's going to try to push boundaries. He's just trying to find his way," she said.

"Oh, he pushing boundaries all right."

"Honey, give the boy some space. We can talk to him in the morning before he goes to school."

Dr. Reynolds scowled for a moment, and then he took a deep breath. "We are going to definitely talk in the morning, Rahim. I assure you."

Kasia touched the temple of her glasses. Rahim's room came into view. Iago was hovering above Rahim's bed.

Kasia's fingers flew over her tablet. She lowered the volume on Iago's speaker.

"Shut down your propellers. Set your alarm for seven a.m., Iago." The drone lowered itself to Rahim's bed and went into sleep mode. Kasia yawned. She was about to go into sleep mode herself. Between trying to break into the two remaining satellites and keeping Rahim's parents from finding out he was in the past, she was exhausted. She closed her laptop and shut down her two other computers and the tablet. She touched the temple on her glasses again, and her equipment started to shimmer until it seemed to disappear. She had incorporated Iago's cloaking tech into her equipment just in case those goofy men in the gray suits came back.

There was knock at her door.

"Hey, Button, is it okay if I come in?"

"Yeah, Dad. I'm not taking over the world right now," Kasia said.

Her father came in the room and squatted in front of Kasia so they were eye to eye, which she knew was hard for him since he was so tall. He placed one hand on her head, gently palmed it like a basketball, and gave it a little shake. Kasia laughed and her dad smiled.

"Hey, I wanted to check on you before you go to bed. I talked to your uncle, and he thinks we should be able to get your stuff back in a few weeks. How's that sound?"

"That's sounds like a plan," Kasia said.

"Look, I know today was kinda scary, but I want you to know that no matter what happens, your mom and I will always support you. You're a special girl and we won't ever let anyone dull your shine. Do you understand me?"

"I know that, Dad. You don't have to get all mushy."

"Girl, all we do is mushy in this house. All right, get to sleep. Before you know it, you'll have your computers back and you'll probably build a shrink ray or something."

"Shrink rays aren't practical. The gravitational differential—"

Her dad chuckled.

"It was a joke, Button. Good night." Her dad kissed her on her forehead before heading down the stairs.

Kasia got into bed and pulled the covers up to her chin.

"I mean, I could probably compensate for the gravity difference—wait, no—I gotta concentrate on getting Ra home."

Sometimes she imagined her brain was like a train station with ideas coming and going every five minutes. Kasia closed her eyes and tried to will herself to sleep. She had to stay on the train that would bring Rahim back home.

RAHIM HAD TO KEEP reminding himself that Grandpa Sam and Ms. Lottie were not his grandparents . . . yet.

Grandpa Sam had fished out a pile of blankets and a pillow for him to sleep on the floor of Omar's bedroom. The next morning, Rahim awoke to the smell of bacon and toast as his not-yet-grandfather cooked breakfast before heading to work.

"Look who's still here—our little houseguest," Ms. Lottie said as she joined them for breakfast. She smiled at Rahim. Between that smile and the huge pile of scrambled eggs Grandpa Sam heaped on his plate, Rahim felt like he was back at his grandparents' house for the summer.

"When I get home tonight, we gonna take another run at finding his people," Grandpa Sam said, breaking the spell.

"That's fine. But right now, I gotta go to sleep. We had a long night. Lots of trains running late. Save me some eggs." Ms. Lottie headed to the living room and sprawled across the couch.

Grandpa Sam grabbed his thermos and his lunch box from the counter. "You boys make sure you wash the dishes. Don't leave that for your mama. And don't let Cy eat up all the eggs. I'll see you tonight."

When he was gone, Shaka focused on Rahim and said, "All right, tell the truth. You ran away from home, didn't you?" Rahim was about to stammer out an answer when Shaka's face blurred in front of him and the whole world seemed to tremble like he was locked inside a salt shaker.

"You okay, Ronald?" Omar asked.

"Yeah, yeah, I'm fine. And I'm not a runaway. Not really."

"Whatever. Help me clean up. I'm going down to the basketball courts," Shaka said.

"Can we come too?" Omar asked.

"You can do whatever you want, but I ain't babysitting you two. You better ask Mama if you can go, though," Shaka said, clearing the table. He started washing the dishes and handing them to Omar to dry. Rahim put the dishes away. When they were done, Shaka went upstairs to get his basketball shorts and shoes.

Omar walked into the living room. Standing a foot away from his mom's head, he whispered softly, "Mama, can me and Ronald go with Shaka to the basketball court?"

His mother responded with a throaty grumble. Omar

stepped back and elbowed Rahim in the arm.

"All right, we're good to go," Omar said.

"You sure about that? Didn't sound like she said any-thing to me," Rahim said.

"Nah, we're good. Let's go."

The basketball court was packed by the time they got there. Shaka high-fived some kids he knew from the neighborhood, and they formed a three-person team.

"We got next!" Shaka called before practicing his dribbling. He bounced the ball effortlessly from one hand to the other, between his legs and behind his back. Rahim and Omar leaned against the chain-link fence that surrounded the court. Omar's necktie flapped in the wind.

"He's really good," Rahim said, motioning to Shaka.

"Yeah. My pop says he is wasting his time playing for the school, but I think Shaka could go pro if he wanted to."

Rahim frowned. He couldn't remember if his uncle had ever said anything about wanting to play pro ball. Was this another change to the timeline? He'd seen that weird blur thing around Shaka's head at breakfast.

Rahim felt his phone vibrate and pulled it out. The green power light was not nearly as bright as it had been yesterday. Kasia's number was on the screen. Rahim walked away from the fence. Once he was sure he was far enough away that Omar couldn't hear him talking, he answered the phone.

"Tell me you got it all fixed," Rahim said.

"You really have to work on your manners when you answer the phone," Kasia said.

"I'm sorry. How's things with you? You good? How's Iago? Now, when can I come home?"

"Well, we're closer today than we were yesterday. The communication satellite was a piece of cake. The teleportation system was kinda hard, but I just got it. That's why I called. Be careful what you look up on the phone because that system is live again. Now, we just gotta get the temporal-wave satellite online and you can come home."

"Thank goodness. Hey, can I ask you a question?" Rahim said.

"As long as it ain't when I'm gonna be done, go ahead," Kasia said.

"What do you think the government was doing with all this stuff? This temporal-wave thing or whatever you called it. Like, it couldn't have been something good, right? It doesn't feel like it was something good," Rahim said.

"I don't know. I think they been trying to get it to

work for a long time. I just kinda beat them to it. Listen, don't worry about that now. Are you at least trying not to talk to anyone?" Kasia asked.

"I'm trying," he said, his throat tightening. "Really, K."

"Uh-huh."

"I am!"

"Don't cry, geez. I'm just trying to make sure you don't change something that will lead to me not making the phone. If that happens, you're stuck," Kasia said.

Rahim swallowed hard. "You really think that could happen?"

Kasia didn't respond immediately. "Look, I'm not trying to scare you, but we are dealing with really serious stuff here. Like super-duper-serious change-the-world stuff."

Now it was Rahim's turn to be quiet. The idea that he might not get home—let alone cause the world to change—hadn't really entered his mind until this exact moment. He just assumed Kasia would fix the whole time-travel thing the way she had fixed the X-ray glasses. It had never dawned on him that maybe this situation was beyond even her impressive capabilities.

"Okay, I hear you, K."

"All right. I'm gonna get back to it. Hey, don't worry about your parents. I got Iago in your room pretending to be you. You're real sick with horrible diarrhea."

"Wait, what?" Rahim asked.

"Later," Kasia said. She ended the call. Rahim shook his head and walked over to the bench where Omar was now sitting.

"Hey, you wanna hit the library?" Omar asked. Rahim put the phone back in his pocket.

"I thought we were gonna watch Shaka play?" Rahim asked.

"He did. While you were on the phone. Now he's gone to hang out with his girlfriend, Tisha."

Rahim scanned the basketball court. There were only a few people milling around. A couple of guys were playing H-O-R-S-E.

"Wait, how long was I on the phone?" Rahim asked.

"Shaka played three games to twenty-one. I guess an hour. I didn't want to bother you. I thought it might be important," Omar said. Rahim leaned against the fence. What was happening? He could have sworn he'd only talked to Kasia for five minutes at the most. It seemed as usual she was right. Him being in the past was changing the way time passed.

It's like a record skipping. You're skipping in and out of this time stream.

Rahim blinked his eyes. That thought wasn't his. It was like it had been whispered into his ear. He wiped his eyes with the back of his hand. When he was done, he saw the figure in the metallic-green coat and face mask standing on the basketball court. The figure nodded at him. Rahim closed his eyes tight. When he opened them again, the figure was gone.

"That is bad. It's real bad," Rahim murmured.

"Huh?" Omar asked.

"Nothing. Yeah, let's get out of here," Rahim said.

They left the court and headed up the street. They skirted around a few slow-moving adults. The breeze kept catching Omar's tie, so he tucked it in his shirt pocket.

"Why does your dad make you wear a tie but not Shaka?"

"He doesn't make me wear neckties. I like them. They make me look unique," Omar said.

Rahim stifled a laugh. That sounded like something his dad would say.

They were just about to reach the corner in front of the library when they heard a voice that froze them in their tracks.

"Reynolds, I think I'm going to take your ugly shoes until you get me my Jordans," Tyrone yelled.

Rahim and Omar turned to face him.

"What?" they said in unison.

Tyrone grinned. He looked like a shark smiling.

"You heard me. Take off your shoes."

His two sidekicks, who were present and accounted for, tittered like hyenas.

"His shoes are not gonna fit your feet," Rahim said. He didn't mean for it to sound like an insult. He was actually making an honest observation. As soon as the words left his mouth, though, he realized his mistake.

Tyrone's face twisted into a ferocious scowl. "What you say?" he asked.

"I—I was just saying . . . um, I believe in you. You can do it. You can wear his shoes," Rahim said.

The two sidekicks stopped laughing, and Tyrone's scowl morphed from a look of confusion to a mask of rage.

"Run!" Omar shouted. Rahim didn't need to be told twice. He took off. Omar sailed past him as they flew down the sidewalk dodging startled pedestrians. Rahim could hear Tyrone and his boys pounding the pavement behind them. Rahim followed Omar as he took a right turn into an alley between two crumbling buildings. His tie flapped like a flag in a windstorm.

"Oh man," Omar said.

The alley was a dead end. Rahim turned just in time to see Tyrone and his cronies closing the distance between them. He twisted his head and saw Omar try-ing to climb the tall wooden fence that closed off the alley. Rahim turned back around, and Tyrone grabbed him by his shirt collar.

"You think you're funny?" Tyrone said.

"No, I really wasn't trying to be funny," Rahim said. "And I'm sure you have wonderful feet."

"I'm gonna knock your head off!" Tyrone yelled. He reared back with his right hand and balled it into a fist. Rahim shut his eyes and braced for the blow. Just then a voice echoed in the alley.

"Hey, what's going on here!?"

A policeman was standing at the mouth of the alley. He had one hand resting on the butt of his pistol. All of the boys froze. "You let him go and come down here. All of you line up against the wall."

Tyrone let Rahim go, and Omar climbed down off the fence. They lined up along the wall facing the policeman.

"Now, what's going on here?" the cop asked. He was a thin man with a narrow face and a prominent Adam's apple that bobbed up and down as he spoke.

No one spoke a word.

"All right, don't everyone talk at once. I'm gonna ask again. What's going on here?"

No one said a thing.

"Okay, that's fine. Let's see if you talk downtown." The policeman grabbed the radio speaker attached to his shoulder and mumbled into it.

"We wasn't doing anything," Tyrone said.

The cop wheeled around and pointed at him. "No, don't talk now. You had your chance."

Rahim had never gone "downtown." He'd never been in trouble with the police. He was scared, but not just for himself. Getting arrested seemed like something that would definitely throw his dad's timeline out of whack.

Think! Think! Rahim thought. He raised his hand.

"Oh, you gonna tell me what happened?" the policeman asked.

"I have a cell phone. I'd like to call my parents," Rahim said.

"How'd a kid like you get a cell phone?"

"My friend got it for me."

"Oh yeah? Let me see it," the policeman said.

Dang it, Rahim thought. He fished the cell phone out of his pocket. As he was about to hand it to the policeman, one of Tyrone's sidekicks made a break for it.

"Hey, stop!" The policeman took off after the sidekick, but a patrol car skidded to a stop in front of the alley, cutting off the fleeing boy.

"What's your address?" Rahim said to Omar.

"What?"

"Your address!" Rahim said. Kasia would be ticked if she knew he was doing exactly what she'd asked him not to do, but he had to get his dad out of here.

"Nine-four-four Sullivan Street," Omar whispered.

Rahim typed in the address and pressed SEND. But not before grabbing Omar's arm.

"What—" Omar started to say.

"—are you doing?" Omar finished.

Rahim put his phone back in his pocket.

Omar turned around in slow circle, his jaw dropped. He stared at Rahim, his eyes as big as dinner plates. They were back in his room. "H-how . . . how did we get back here?" Omar asked.

"My phone gets a lot better reception than you'd think," Rahim offered.

13

KASIA SAT ON THE counter as her mom and dad helped their customers pick their cucumbers, tomatoes, and peppers. They were at the co-op her parents had designed and built in an old warehouse four blocks from their house. Outside it was still ice-cube cold, but in the warehouse the high-power reflective lamps and the powerful geothermal heat pump system kept the temperature a balmy ninety degrees. Kasia was actually sweating. She yawned. She had stayed up late trying to get Rahim home. After getting her equipment back yesterday, she had worked nearly all night. When her mom had woken her up this morning, it felt like she had just gone to bed.

The chime on the front door rang.

Agent Brown and Agent Green walked through the door, still wearing their identical gray suits and sunglasses. They stood by the cash register as her mom rang up Mr. Khan's huge bag of peppers.

Kasia's dad walked over to the counter. "Can I help you, gentlemen?"

The two agents both folded their arms across their chests. "We'd like to ask your daughter how she stole back her computer equipment," Agent Green said.

"What are you talking about?" her dad asked.

"Your daughter's equipment disappeared from our vehicle. We'd like to ask her how she did it and where it is," Agent Brown said.

Her dad crossed his arms. "So, what you're telling me is, you lost her property?" he said.

Agent Brown and Agent Green didn't respond.

"You lost her stuff and now you come in here accusing her of stealing it? What kind of people do that to a little girl?" Mrs. Collins said.

"You guys are picking on a little girl? For shame!" Mr. Khan said.

"I can't believe this! You're blaming this little girl for your incompetence!" Mrs. Testaverde said. She shook a cucumber at the two agents. Soon a crowd of customers were surrounding the agents, who were beginning to back up toward the door.

"You know what? I don't think you should come back here. From now on, if you want to contact us, you can do it through our lawyer. He will be back from Australia the day after tomorrow," Dad said.

"I bet your mothers don't like the way you treat little kids!" Mrs. Testaverde said. The agents were sweating, but Kasia was pretty sure it wasn't just from the heat. As they backed out of the front door, she waved to them and smiled.

When the agents had left, her mom hugged her. "You okay?" she asked.

"Yeah, Mom, I'm fine. It's no big."

Her mom looked over her shoulder at her dad, who was talking to Mr. Khan.

"Okay, then. I guess we can tell your uncle not to worry about getting your equipment back, since you already got it," her mom said.

Kasia felt her mouth open wide. "How did you know?"

"I didn't. But now I do. My little princess. You're a brilliant girl, but mothers know their children. I saw that sassy wave you gave those agents."

"You're not mad?"

"Mad? Nah. I'm just a tiny bit sad you felt like you couldn't tell us. But mad? No, those agents tried to bully you, and they got just what they deserve. We'll wait a little while and tell your dad. Sometimes he likes to be riled up. We'll let him get it out of his system."

"I'm sorry, Mom. I should've told you."

"It's okay as long as there's nothing else you're holding back. Like, how exactly did you get your equipment back?" her mom asked with an arch of her eyebrows.

Kasia almost said it. She almost let it all out in one

long breath. *I built Rahim a phone and hacked some government stuff and accidentally sent him back in time and now I'm trying to bring him home before he does damage to the timeline.*

But . . .

She didn't. She had to do this herself. Even if her parents believed her, they wouldn't be able to help. They'd just tell Ra's parents and then they would all just get in her way.

"No, Mom, nothing you need to worry about. And, well . . . I used Iago to get my stuff back," Kasia said finally. Her mom smiled.

"My brilliant little girl. Come on, help me stock the cucumbers before you change the world," her mom said as she gave her a hug.

They spent the rest of the day working on the growing beds, helping customers and members of the co-op, and picking their own vegetables for dinner. All the while, Kasia kept thinking about Rahim. Was he keeping to himself like she told him? How would she know if he wasn't? If he was changing things in the past, she wouldn't know it until she got home and checked the homework she had saved on the computer. And that homework had just been a few assignments about history. What if he did something that changed a scientific discovery? Or worse yet, what if he did something that prevented the satellite grid from being built so that she couldn't make the phone in the first place?

Paradoxes. They were enough to make your head hurt.

Kasia helped her mom dump some of the tomatoes that had gone bad or overripened into the compost bin in the back alley of the warehouse. As they were heading inside, someone standing at the end of the alley in front of the wooden fence caught her attention. The person was tall and slim, and wearing a long purple leather coat over a black one-piece outfit. Their face was hidden by a black helmet. The person in the helmet waved at her. Before she knew what she was doing, Kasia was waving back.

"Kasia, come on. It's freezing out here!" Her mom held open the back door.

Kasia turned her head. "I'm coming, Mom." When she looked back toward the person in the helmet, they were gone. Kasia didn't think they could have climbed the fence that fast, and they hadn't passed her to walk out of the alley.

"Okay, that's weird," she said. Normally, she liked weird. Weird was interesting. But given the current situation with her best friend, weird was now scary.

14

"OKAY, TELL ME AGAIN. Slow this time."

Omar was sitting on his bed. Rahim was sitting in his desk chair. Omar was staring at him like he'd grown a second head.

"I can't tell you too much," Rahim said. "Just know I'm not from around here and this phone can do some crazy stuff."

"No duh. How does it work?" Omar asked.

Rahim scratched his head. "I'm not really sure. I just know I can't talk about it too much."

"It's like that thing on *Star Trek*. Wait, are you from outer space? Like an alien?" Omar asked.

"No. I'm from Philly. Just not your Philly."

Omar lay back on the bed.

"You know what this means?" Omar asked.

"That we have to keep it a secret while I figure out how to get home?"

Omar sat up straight. "No. It means we can get into the Four the Hard Way concert tonight!"

Rahim squinted at Omar. "Have you heard anything I've been saying?"

"Yeah, I heard you. You got a super phone that can teleport us anywhere. Where else would you rather be tonight than at the Four the Hard Way concert?" Omar asked.

"Home. I want to go home. Which might not happen if we keep using this thing," Rahim said.

"But you used it today so we could get away from the cop?"

"Yeah, because I didn't want to go to jail. That was an emergency."

"You think I'll ever get a chance to see them again? My dad is talking about sending me to Reading next year to go to a private school. He keeps saying all I should be thinking about is hitting the books. And I do like books. But I like other stuff too. School is important, I know that. But it ain't everything. It can't be."

Rahim studied the ceiling, then the floor. He thought Omar might be crying. He probably didn't want Rahim to see that, and Rahim absolutely didn't want to see that.

It sounded like he and his dad had more in common than he would have thought.

"Okay, we can go. But we have to be super careful. Don't talk to anyone. We only stay for two songs, then we get the heck out of there," Rahim said.

Omar wiped his nose and raised his head.

"For real?"

"Yeah, for real. I'm sure I'll regret it, but yeah, for reals," Rahim said.

"Okay, the show isn't till six. You know how to play chess?" Omar asked.

"Yeah. My dad taught me."

"All right, then prepare for a butt whupping." Omar started to set up the board. Rahim rolled the desk chair over to the bed.

"Is your dad nice, or is he like my dad?" Omar asked.

Rahim frowned.

"I mean, my dad is kinda on it about school like yours, but he's crazy smart. My mom is too. My sister might be, but she doesn't talk to me that much, so I'm not sure," Rahim said.

Omar laughed. "Your sister sounds like Shaka. But you didn't say if your dad was nice." Omar moved his first pawn.

Rahim moved his own pawn.

"I mean, he can be. One time we went to New York to visit some guy he'd gone to college with and he took us to Central Park and we all went rollerblading. My dad was, like, a genius at blading. He was doing tricks and stuff. But when we got home, he went back to being the same old dad. I don't know. It's like he forgot he was a professor when we were up there," Rahim said. That he was saying all this to the boy who would one day become his dad made him feel awkward. Would his dad remember this conversation? Would he remember talking to a kid who told him about rollerblading in New York? Was his dad good at rollerblading because he'd talked to Rahim in the past?

Rahim shook his head. If he kept thinking about things like that, he'd have to take a nap.

"Knight takes pawn," Omar said.

Rahim looked at the board. Omar was trying to set him up for a Fool's Mate. Rahim moved his rook. "Rook takes knight. Check," he said.

Omar looked at the board, then at Rahim, and then back at the board. "Your dad must be a good chess player," Omar said dejectedly.

"He wasn't always," Rahim said. A slight smile played across his face.

KASIA SAT AT HER computer and let her fingers fly over the keyboard like bees buzzing around a rosebush. The screen seemed to melt into a never-ending series of flashing lights. As she worked, an alert from Iago blinked on the screen embedded in the right lens of her glasses.

"Hmm . . . they're knocking at his door again? Let's see if this gets their attention." Kasia stopped working on her desktop computer and grabbed the tablet that was connected to Iago. She moved her finger over the screen and the sound of a ringing phone filled her room.

"Hello?" Dr. Reynolds said.

"Hi, Dad. I'm spending the night at . . . Tariq's house," Rahim's voice said.

"Now, just hold on a minute. Your mom and I haven't seen you for a whole day. And who is Tariq? You need to come home, and I mean with extreme expeditiousness," Dr. Reynolds said.

"Tariq is my . . . friend. I'll be home . . . tomorrow," the simulation said.

"Boy, if you don't get your—"

Kasia ended the call. "I hope when I get you home your dad doesn't ground you for the rest of the year." And she went back to working on her computer.

As she broke down firewalls and rerouted security trackers, the memory of the person from the alley came to her like a dream. The way they had waved at her and then just—well—just disappeared bothered Kasia. She hated being fooled. She had once reduced a street magician to tears because she kept telling everyone gathered how his tricks worked.

She'd been six.

Maybe Helmet Head was coming into her life now because of something Rahim had done in the past. But if that was the case, why didn't they introduce themselves to Kasia? The way they had just stared at her from the back of the alley had been creepy.

I hope you're taking this seriously, Rahim. Because I think things could get real bad if you don't, Kasia thought.

16

RAHIM HOPED HE WASN'T messing up the timeline too bad. He and Omar were eating dinner with Uncle Cy and Shaka. Ms. Lottie had left for work and Grandpa Sam hadn't gotten home yet, so Cy had made dinner.

"I hope you like frank and beans because that's all I know how to cook," Cy said as he spooned hard, burned bits of beans and franks onto their plates.

"I mean, I ain't no chef, but are frank and beans supposed to be crunchy?" Shaka asked.

"Hey, I didn't see you volunteering to put nothing on the table." Cy sat down and began to shovel forkfuls of crunchy beans into his mouth. Rahim thought Cy knew the beans were awful but was determined not to admit it.

"I'm out." Shaka got up from the table.

"Hey, where you going?" Cy asked.

"I'm going over to Tisha's to see if her mama got anything I can actually eat."

"Suit yourself," Cy said. He put another forkful in his

mouth and grimaced. Rahim tried to eat too, but it felt like he was trying to chew dice. Omar wasn't even trying. He just tapped his foot on the floor and his fork on his plate. He hadn't touched one bite of his food.

Rahim knew he was excited about going to the show, but he wished he would turn it down a notch. If Grandpa Sam got home soon, Rahim was sure he'd pick up on Omar's excitement and start to question them. The next thing they knew, he'd give them that look that all dads give, telling them to go to bed.

Maybe that's what we should be doing, Rahim thought. As much as he wanted to do something nice for his dad—er . . . Omar—to make him happy, he kept thinking about what Kasia had said. What if what he did tonight caused him to be trapped in the past forever?

"You gonna eat that?" Cy asked. He pointed a fork at Rahim's plate.

"I don't think so."

Omar said, "Come on, let's go to my room. Let me get a rematch."

"More for me," Cy said as he dumped the contents of Rahim's plate onto his own.

Rahim followed Omar upstairs to his room.

"I got some pillows from the closet. We can put them under the covers in case my parents check on us during the night," Omar said. He gestured to the pillows that were sitting in a pile at the foot of the bed and smiled. Rahim could tell he was proud of himself.

"What if they actually come in the room for a closer look?" Rahim asked. Omar shook his head.

"They never do that," Omar said.

"First, I don't believe that. Second, what if this is the one night they decide to do just that?" Rahim said.

Omar ignored him and shoved the pillows under the blankets. Once he was done, he sat on the edge of his bed and frowned at Rahim.

"Are you scared? Like, if you're scared, tell me how to work the phone and I'll go by myself."

"I'm not scared. Not really. I'm just saying do we have a backup plan," Rahim said.

"Sounds like something a scaredy-cat would say."

"I'm not a—"

"Scaredddy-caaaat," Omar sang.

"I'm not a—"

"Scaredddy-caaaat—"

Rahim pulled out the phone. He typed in the address of the performance hall. Without saying a word, he grabbed Omar by the shoulder, and pressed ENTER.

Just before the watery sensation washed over them, he heard Mr. Reynolds's voice calling to them from the hallway.

DOWNSTAIRS, KASIA'S MOTHER WAS sitting in the living room with Mrs. Reynolds. Kasia immediately turned around and headed back up the stairs.

"Kasia, come here," her mom said.

"Sure, Mom."

When she walked into the living room, Mrs. Reynolds smiled at her, but it seemed weak. It never reached her eyes.

"Kasia, do you know where Rahim is?" her mom asked.

"I thought he was at home," Kasia said. She didn't look at her mother or Mrs. Reynolds.

"I know you two are good friends. I think you guys look out for each other. I love that. I really do. But today I went into his room, and it hasn't been slept in for days. He called this afternoon and said he was staying with someone named Tariq, but we called some of his classmates and there's no Tariq in his class. My husband is out looking for him right now, Kasia," Mrs. Reynolds said.

"I know you don't want to get him in trouble, but we really need to know where he is, honey." Her eyes were red, and she was squeezing a tissue in her right hand. Kasia thought maybe she should tell her the truth. But she realized she had no way to prove that Rahim had gone back in time. Even if she called him and had him talk to his mom, it was just a voice on the other end of a phone.

"If I hear from him, I will tell him to call you, Mrs. Reynolds," Kasia said. She lowered her head and studied her shoes.

"Okay. If he calls you, let him know we are not angry. We just want him to come home." She got up and gave Kasia's mom a hug before going out the back door.

"Kasia," her mom said, and patted the sofa cushion next to her.

She plopped down beside her mom.

"You know, when we decided to homeschool you, we knew it was going to be a challenge. You're so smart, Button, and to be honest, I think you're gonna be in college in just a couple years. We debated a long time about whether we should homeschool you or not. We were worried you would miss out on making friends. Then you and Rahim became best buds. You guys help each other out a lot. Now, I know you might think you're helping him out, but if you know where he is or where he might be, you need to tell us. That's how you really help him."

Kasia scuffed the toe of her sneaker against the wood floor. "I built Rahim a phone that accidentally sent him back in time, and now I'm trying to get him home."

Her mom tapped her index finger against her lips before she spoke. "So, this is like the X-ray specs again," her mom said.

"Yeah," Kasia said. "Maybe a little worse."

Her mom rubbed her palms over her knees before clapping her hands together. "All right. What do we need to do to get him home?" Mom asked.

"You believe me?"

"Kasia, if there is one thing I've learned since I was lucky enough to become your mother, it is to not underestimate you." She put her arm around Kasia and pulled her close. "Now, what do we need to do?"

"Honestly, Mom? I just need some space."

"Okay. Okay, we can get you all the space you need. You can get him back, right, Button?"

"Yeah . . . as long as he is doing exactly what I told him to do," Kasia said.

She hoped Rahim wasn't doing what she told him not to, though.

THE FIRST THING RAHIM heard when they appeared in the audience was the screams of the girls standing next to him. He heard them over the pre-recorded music that was playing while the crowd waited for the group to arrive.

"Aaargh! Raynathan, there's ghosts in here!" a girl cried.

Rahim noticed the guy standing next to her was bigger than him and Omar combined. Rahim pushed Omar along just as the massive man was turning his head their way.

"What is wrong with you, Bianca? Ain't no such thing as ghosts," Raynathan said.

"I'm telling you, one minute there wasn't nobody there, and then the next minute two kids were standing right next to me."

Rahim and Omar posted up next to the exit once they had worked their way through the crowd. Rahim had a brief moment where he was shocked the crowd was so small. Then he remembered it was 1997 and Four the Hard Way were just getting started. They wouldn't hit their prime for a few more years.

"I can't believe we're at a Four the Hard Way concert. This is gonna be the greatest night of my life!" Omar yelled.

"Yeah, as long as we don't get caught," Rahim said.

"Will you stop worrying? You got a magic phone. Like, it literally got us inside a concert with no tickets!"

"First of all, it's not magic. And don't say that so loud. You wanna get us kicked out?" Rahim asked.

"Who cares? We'll just come back in again!" Omar smiled broadly.

"I don't know if that would be a good idea. I have to be careful how I use this thing until I can get home. I've already changed some stuff that didn't need to be changed," Rahim said.

"What do you mean, you changed some stuff? Wait, are you from the future?!" Omar asked.

"Huh? Did I say that? No, I'm not from the future. What are you talking about?" Rahim craned his neck toward the stage. He hoped Four the Hard Way would come out to start their show and save him from answering any of Omar's questions.

"Yeah, you are! Oh man, tell me! Do I go to college? Do I make a rap album? Do the Sixers ever win another title? Do I get a girlfriend?" Omar's questions shot out fast like pellets from a paint gun. Rahim did his best to dodge them.

"I'm not from the future, and even if I was, I couldn't tell you. So you can just stop asking," Rahim said.

"Does that phone tell you what happens in the future?" Omar asked.

Just as Rahim was trying to come up with an answer that didn't endanger the space-time continuum, the lights in the concert hall began to dim. The crowd erupted as the first notes of Four the Hard Way's hit "The Lords of the Flow" rumbled through the sound system. Rahim felt the excitement of the crowd cascade over them like a tidal wave.

"Are you ready???" a disembodied voice asked. "Here they are, Too Smooth, Rock G, MC Juice, and the Sultan. Get ready for the ruckus! Here comes FOUR—THE—HARD—WAY!!!" The lights flashed on as a trio of dancers bounded onto the stage followed by all four members of the group.

MC Juice roared, "We can rock fast or we can rock slow. It don't really matter cuz we the Lords of the Flow!"

Rahim knew Juice always led off the group's songs because of his deep voice.

Rahim felt his phone vibrating. He pulled it out of his pocket. There was no way he would be able to hear

Kasia with the music blaring out of the speakers.

Gonna have to get back to you, K, he thought. As he pushed the END button on the phone, a kid wearing a FOUR THE HARD WAY T-shirt jumped into the air. When he came down, he slammed into Rahim's back. The phone jumped out of his hand and skittered across the floor into the darkness of the crowd and their thunderous feet stomping in time with the music.

19

THE FIRST THING KASIA thought was that Rahim was in someone's car. There was a noise like traffic on Market Street on the other end of the line. Music and shouting rang in her ears.

"Rahim, where are you?" Kasia asked.

"Huh? Who dis?" a voice said.

Kasia almost smacked herself in the head. That wasn't Rahim. The voice on the other end of the line was deep and husky.

"Who are you?" Kasia asked.

"Who going to the zoo?" the voice asked.

"No, WHO ARE YOU?" Kasia yelled into her mic.

"Josh. Who dis?" Josh asked.

"Where is Rahim?" Kasia yelled.

Josh didn't respond. She heard more yelling and more music. The beat seemed familiar, but she couldn't place it. Kasia heard the muffled roar of a crowd. She thought she could hear the phone clatter to the floor. There was a dizzying moment as the sound from the phone seemed to spiral out of control.

"Rahim, what have you done?" Kasia said.

Rahim tried to push his way through the crowd as he followed the phone, but he was bounced around like a balloon. He bumped into a pair of girls with thick braids and huge, dangling gold earrings. They in turn pushed him into a couple of guys who were trying to perform an elaborate dance routine that involved kicks, jumps, and a particularly ridiculous shimmy. Rahim squinted his eyes and tried to focus on the electric-blue phone case. It was bouncing across the floor like a hockey puck. He watched in horror as a big guy picked it up and put it to his ear.

"Oh man, come on!" Rahim said.

A kid next to him clapped him on the back. "Ain't they fly?" he said.

Rahim slipped between two people dancing as he made his way toward the guy holding his phone. A couple of girls started dancing with the big guy. In his excitement, he juggled the big bulky device and it fell from his hand. Rahim took off running, spinning, and diving around people, sliding across the floor on his knees. He caught the phone in both hands like it was a baby before it hit the ground.

"Gotcha!" Rahim exclaimed.

A strange sound filled the auditorium like a long-extended groan. Rahim shoved the phone back in his pocket. He started to rise to his feet when someone next to him shouted a warning.

"Oh snap!"

Rahim raised his head. He was right in front of the stage. And right in front of him was the Sultan, dressed in a pair of baggy black jeans, a Raiders jersey, and a red turban. He dropped down to his haunches and was holding a microphone in front of Rahim's face. The beat from the song was roaring from the speakers like a stampede of wild horses.

"Sing it!" the Sultan yelled.

Without missing a beat, Rahim screamed into the mic, "We can rock fast or we can rock slow. It don't really matter cuz we the Lords of the Flow!"

The crowd erupted. The whole building seemed to shake and tremble.

I'm actually seeing Four the Hard Way live in person with my dad, Rahim thought. A huge grin spilled across his face. For the first time since he'd picked up that crazy phone, he wasn't scared or sad or wondering what was happening. For a moment, he was just enjoying an incredible show by his favorite group with a kid who was his dad but had become his friend.

Omar found him and slugged his shoulder.

"This is awesome!" he said.

"Yeah, it really is."

20

KASIA KNEW SOMETHING WAS wrong the minute she heard her dad's voice. It had that same high whistling tone as the time he got cornered by a gigantic spider in the bathroom.

Kasia got up from her computer and went to the top of the stairs.

"What the heck is this in the backyard?" her dad said. The pitch of his voice climbed higher. Something about the way he was yelling made Kasia nervous.

She ran downstairs and into the kitchen. The back door was wide open, and a frigid wind was filling the house. Kasia went to the door and poked her head outside. The cold air made her wince, but it was what she saw that made her gasp.

Her dad was holding a bag of trash. Obviously, he'd been taking the trash out, but now that was going to be impossible. Kasia watched as the wind lifted their large blue trash can. The can paused for a moment above the hole before disappearing into the darkness.

"Is it a sinkhole?" her mom asked. She was standing

just behind her father at the bottom of the porch steps. Her flowing wrap swirled in the cold breeze. Her dad took two steps backward.

"I don't think so. It's not actually in the ground," her dad said.

Kasia could see what her dad meant by the hole not being in the ground. She could see the frozen ground beneath the hole. The hole floated above the ground. Its interior was a swirling darkness, as if someone had pulled the drain on a sink full of ink. The edges of the hole were fuzzy and blurry. The hole itself was only about a foot above the ground and about three feet wide. Just wide enough to swallow their trash can.

"Uh-oh," Kasia said. Her parents turned in unison.

"Button, you wouldn't know anything about this, would you?" her dad said. Kasia looked at her mom. Her mom nodded.

"I think it might be a vortex," Kasia said.

"A what?" her dad asked.

"A spontaneously produced wormhole. And I think I know where it came from," she said. "And I think it won't be the last one we see."

"Does this have something to do with where Rahim went?" he asked.

"Let's go inside, and we can all talk about this," her mom said.

"Yeah. Yeah, let's do that," her dad said. He backed away from the vortex with short, measured movements. Once he reached the steps, he stopped and tossed the trash bag toward the vortex. Just like the trash can, the bag paused for a moment before being sucked down into . . . the nothing inside the hole.

Her dad seemed like he was in a trance. "That's not good, is it, Button?"

"No, Dad. I don't think it's good at all. It's about as far from good as cold is from hot."

Her dad hurried up the steps and gently guided her mom through the door. Over her parents' shoulders,

she saw the person in the helmet. They were standing a few feet away from the vortex, arms crossed. The purple trench coat seemed to ripple in the wind like a flag. They gave Kasia a quick shake of their head.

Then they were gone.

The person didn't start to glow and then disappear. They didn't start to fade away like a cheap CGI effect. One minute, they were there. The next minute, gone.

Her parents were waiting for her in the living room on the couch. Her dad was still eyeing the back door nervously as she walked out of the kitchen. Kasia sat down on the ottoman in front of them.

"Guess I should start at the beginning. But I'll go fast because I don't know how much time we have," Kasia said.

"How much time for what?" Dad asked.

"I don't know how much time we have before our universe and its timeline starts folding in on itself and vanishes from existence," Kasia said.

Her dad rubbed his temples. "I shouldn't have asked. Okay, start from the beginning and then tell us what we need to do. And, Button? Don't leave out anything."

Kasia nodded. "I won't. I don't how much you're gonna believe, though," Kasia said.

"When it comes to you, I'll believe almost anything."

21

OMAR AND RAHIM JOINED the crowd of people that had spilled out onto the sidewalk. Everyone was laughing and singing and dancing. The concert had ended ten minutes earlier, but the positive vibe was still strong. Rahim felt like he was at the best birthday party he'd ever been to.

"Man, that was the best thing that has ever happened to me in my whole life," Omar said. He and Rahim had moved to the edge of the sidewalk as the crowd moved down the street.

"Yeah, it was bussin'," Rahim said.

Omar squinted at him.

"Means it was awesome," Rahim said. And just like that, he was snapped back to reality. He was a time-traveling kid stuck in the past with his dad at a concert. A concert that was famous for—

"Hey, we should try to get some autographs before they leave. They park the bands' buses around the corner," Omar said. He took off without waiting for Rahim to respond.

"Hey, wait up!" But Omar was already near the tour bus, his tie trailing behind like a streamer. There was a large group of fans waiting at the rear entrance of the hall. Many of them had posters or CDs. Rahim and Omar were at the back of the pack.

"We're never gonna get close enough for an autograph," Rahim said.

"You should use your phone," Omar whispered.

"It's not a toy." Rahim almost passed out because that was something his dad would have said back home.

"I'm just saying. You could get us closer," he whispered.

Rahim was about to tell Omar for the second time that the phone was not a toy when several things happened at once. The rear door opened and Four the Hard Way started filing out of the building. The crowd burst into applause.

At the end of the block, a car turned onto the street where the tour bus was parked. The driver must've been in a hurry because the vehicle was flying. The street was a one-way, and despite the large group of fans on the sidewalk, the driver had plenty of room to get around the bus. That was until a huge blue plastic trash can dropped from the sky onto the street right in front of the car. The driver tried to slam on the brakes, but that just made the car lurch to the right.

In the five seconds between the car turning down the street and the trash can appearing from nowhere, Rahim remembered something unique about the concert.

Wait a minute. This is the concert where the Sultan broke his leg, Rahim thought. He'd read about the incident in old issues of the *Philadelphia Inquirer* at the library. The Sultan got hit by a car and broke his leg. He dropped out of the tour and eventually left the group. They had already recorded their third album, which would eventually cement their legacy, but two years after the accident, Four the Hard Way would break up.

As the car skidded up onto the sidewalk, the crowd scattered like leaves. Rahim and Omar jumped off the sidewalk into the street.

"Sultan, look out!" Rahim yelled so loud he made himself jump. The Sultan propelled himself backward and disappeared inside the hall as the car careened past the doorway, missing everyone, and ran into a wall. The driver stumbled out, stunned, but he seemed okay.

Silence filled the night. No one was quite sure what to say or do. Then the Sultan reappeared in the doorway. The autograph seekers started clapping and hollering.

The Sultan made a big production out of wiping his forehead. "Man, he almost got me. But a king is too quick to go out like that." A couple of large men rushed to his side.

"And where was y'all at?" the Sultan asked.

"Sorry, boss, we got caught up at the concession stand."

The Sultan shook his head and pointed toward Rahim and Omar. "If it hadn't been for them young bucks over there, I would have been flat as Grandma's pancakes. If you wasn't my cousins, I'd fire both of you."

"Sorry, Stanley," one of the men said.

The Sultan rolled his eyes. "It's the Sultan when we in public, Herbie."

"Hey, you okay, man?" the Sultan yelled to the driver of the car. The driver was checking out the damage to his vehicle but stopped to give the Sultan a thumbs-up.

"Herbie, go over there and give him some free tickets to the next show. His car is messed up. He's having a bad week."

"But he almost hit you," Herbie said.

"It was an accident. Plus, it's good publicity. Go ahead. I'm gonna get on the bus. I'm tired. And where is Juice at?" the Sultan asked.

"He was talking to some fans," Herbie said. The Sultan chuckled. He turned and started to climb on the tour bus.

"WE LOVE YOUR MUSIC!" Omar screamed. He cupped his hands around his mouth and bellowed it. Rahim slapped his forehead. It was one thing to want an autograph. It was another thing to maybe save the Sultan from a broken leg. But it was quite another thing to scream like a fire alarm at the man.

"You guys wanna get a tour of the bus while we wait for Juice?" the Sultan asked. Rahim thought he heard Omar actually squeal.

"Yes, sir!" Omar said.

"We have to get back home!" Rahim whispered.

"Don't we still have the phone? We can be home in less than a second. When are we ever gonna get a chance like this again?" Omar asked. Rahim had to admit it was a one-in-a-lifetime chance.

"Y'all coming?"

Omar was already walking toward the bus. Rahim fell into step behind him, but not before he caught a glimpse of the trash can that had seemed to fall out of the sky.

"Well, that's weird," Rahim said. He paused. The trash can was one of the heavy blue ones that people left on the corner for the garbagemen to pick up way too early in the morning. What made him pause was a series of stick figures painted on the side of the container in a flat red finish.

Rahim knew those stick figures. They were hieroglyphics. Kasia had painted them on her family's trash can last summer. They were based on a system of glyphs she had created for fun one day when she was bored.

If you knew the code, you knew they spelled *Collins*. Rahim bit his bottom lip. He knew those glyphs, but he also knew it was impossible for Kasia's trash can to be sitting in the middle of the street in 1997.

"What is going on?" Rahim said. He took another look at that trash can and felt his stomach drop to his knees.

"Yo, you coming, man?" the Sultan asked again.

Rahim snapped his head toward the Sultan.

"Yeah, I'm coming, sir."

The Sultan laughed. "Yo, man, I ain't no sir."

As they climbed on the bus, a large black bag fell from the sky and landed near the trash can.

22

KASIA'S DAD WAS THE one who decided they shouldn't tell Dr. and Mrs. Reynolds about Rahim going back in time. At least not yet. "They probably won't believe us. Even after the X-ray specs incident. And that will just make them even more upset."

"How much longer do you think it's going to take for you to get him back?" Dad asked.

"Another day at least. Once I crack this last code, I'm in and I can get him back," Kasia said.

"Okay. Then we need to give you the time to do what you have to do. We'll keep those government guys off you, and we'll keep Dr. and Mrs. Reynolds at arm's length until you're done. Now, here's the ten-million-dollar question. If you get Rahim back and fix the . . . What did you call it?"

"The timeline fluctuation," Kasia said.

"Yeah, that. If you fix that, will that get rid of the vortex in the backyard? Because it's getting bigger," her dad said.

"Yeah, yeah, that'll fix it," Kasia said.

Now as Kasia let her fingers fly over her keyboard, well, she wasn't so sure. Getting Rahim back might fix everything. *Might* being the important word. In all honesty she wasn't sure what would happen when they got him home. She wasn't an expert on time travel . . . yet.

Kasia entered the dial command, and Rahim picked up.

"You figured out how to get me out of here yet?" Rahim said.

"I'm working on it. Where are you? Like right this minute?"

Rahim turned on his side and pulled his pillow under his head.

"I'm in my dad's room. He's downstairs. We just got back from what was probably the greatest concert I've ever seen," Rahim said.

"You've never been to a concert before, Rahim. You got nothing to compare it to. Wait, did you go see Four the Hard Way?" Kasia asked.

Rahim sighed. "It's a long story. But my dad—um, Omar—really wanted to go. I mean, I never knew he liked hip-hop, let alone that we had the same favorite group."

"Ra, I know this is all really cool, and I'm glad you and your dad are bonding. But whatever you're doing, you have to stop. The timeline isn't just changing. It's starting to fracture. It's getting corrupted," Kasia said.

"You talking like I'm a Sith Lord. What do you mean corrupted?"

"Ra, there's a temporal vortex in my backyard."

Silence.

"A wormhole. It's like . . . I think maybe whatever you're doing, going back in time, changing things is starting to tear apart the timeline. That's where the hole came from. And it's getting bigger."

"K, this hole you talking about. Did it eat your trash can?" Rahim said.

"Yes! Hold up—how did you know that?"

"I saw it fall out of the sky earlier. I guess that means one of those holes is here. K, what happens if this hole gets really, really big?" Rahim asked.

"I mean, I don't wanna scare you."

"Too late," Rahim said.

"Okay, in theory, if it keeps getting bigger, it could consume the universe. Maybe," Kasia said.

"I think I'm gonna be sick," Rahim said.

"Hey, just chill out, okay? I'm close to getting into the system. I've been bouncing my IP address all over the place so the government agents—"

"What government agents?"

"Never mind that. What I'm saying is, when we get you home, everything should go back to normal. I think."

"I'm not even gonna say anything about that 'I think,'" Rahim said.

"How'd you get in the concert? Did your dad have an extra ticket or something?" Kasia asked.

"I gotta go."

"Rahim, did you use the teleporter? Oh my God, are you trying to send us back to the Stone Age?"

"I'll talk to you later. I hear someone coming." Rahim ended the call.

Kasia sat back in her chair. Iago flew over and landed on her desk. Since Rahim's parents knew he was missing, she'd let Iago come home. No use in having him pretend to be Rahim now.

Kasia swiveled around in her chair and turned on her other computer. She needed a distraction. It was too quiet in her room. She clicked on a video channel. *That's funny,* she thought. She had the strangest feeling there hadn't always been a whole television network channel devoted to the social media video app. She made a mental note to ask Rahim about it later.

She got back to work, but that only lasted for a few minutes. A news report interrupted a clip of a dog doing backflips with sunglasses on.

"Good evening, everyone. I'm Luis Escobedo, and this is a special news report. An enormous sinkhole has opened up near Independence National Historical Park.

Citizens are advised to avoid the area. State and federal officials are on their way to the site."

Kasia's mouth fell open as she listened to the reporter do his best to explain what was happening near the Liberty Bell. A video of the sinkhole played on-screen that had a fuzzy, faraway effect. Most likely it was filmed on a cell phone. This vortex was enormous. At least sixty feet across. Parts of the sidewalk were falling into it, along with some trees and a particularly ugly bench.

Kasia went back to work on her keyboard. Her insides were in knots.

This all got a lot more interesting real quick, Kasia thought. "Come on, Ra, stop changing things long enough for me to get you home. While there's still a home to come back to."

23

OMAR STARTED TO SPEAK, but Grandpa Sam held up his hand. Omar shut his mouth with an audible *plop!*

"I only have two questions. Where have you been, and did you think no one would notice you were gone?" Grandpa Sam's voice was low and quiet, but Rahim could see him clenching and unclenching his hands.

"We went to a concert," Omar mumbled.

"Speak up. When you talk to someone, you speak clearly. You don't mumble."

"We went to the concert," Omar said.

"The concert Shaka went to? Did he take you to that concert?"

"No, sir, Mr. Reynolds," Rahim said.

"I don't recall asking you anything yet, Ronald."

Rahim dropped his head and studied his hands. "Shutting up, sir."

"So, let me see if I got this straight. You and your new friend sneak out of the house. Then you go to a concert with one of them rap groups where they use all kinds of bad language and who knows what is happening in the crowd. Then you sneak back in like a couple of thieves in the night. And if I hadn't have come home early, you probably would have gotten away with it. Is that about it?"

Well, a trash can from the future fell out of the sky, Rahim thought.

"We had fun," Omar murmured.

"What I done told you about speaking up?"

"We had fun! We even got to go on the tour bus," Omar said. His voice was loud and clear.

"You did what? Boy, you better take some of that bass out your voice."

"I'm sorry, Pop, but I had fun. More fun than I've had in a long time. I know you want me to say I'm sorry. I know you want me to be ashamed of sneaking out, but I'm not! I had a good time with my friend. Ronald is pretty much the only friend I have, and tonight was the best night of my life," Omar said.

"You done?" his father asked.

Omar crossed his arms and dropped his head as well.

"I'll tell you what I know. I know you're too young to be on the street at eleven at night. I know you had no business at a show for grown folks. I know you didn't have no business going on some tour bus. I know you think I'm too hard on you, but I definitely know it's for your own good.

And I know one day you're going to thank me for it."

Grandpa Sam pointed at Rahim. "Tomorrow we taking you to social services. I really didn't want to do it, but I can't have you around my boy. You're a bad influence. Now, I'm sorry about your people leaving you, but I just can't have this kind of behavior in my house."

"No, Pop!"

"I'm not gonna tell you about the tone of your voice again, Omar. Now go to sleep. Tomorrow you can write me a six-page essay about why rules and order are important. Good night." He turned on his heel and walked out of the room.

"He's so mean," Omar said.

"He gets nicer," Rahim said, remembering the grandfather he knew.

"What?" Omar asked.

"Nothing. Let's just go to bed."

"You're not mad? He's kicking you out all because we had a good time," Omar said.

"I can't believe I'm gonna say this, but he kinda has a point. I mean, it was a great concert. Better than I even thought it could be—"

"That's what I'm saying!" Omar said.

"But . . . we did sneak out. We did almost got hit by a car. And we were out way too late."

"You're sounding real wack." He stretched out over his bed and faced the wall.

"I'm just saying maybe your dad is right. Me being here probably isn't the best thing ever," Rahim said.

"No, he isn't. He just likes to tell me what to do. He tells everybody what to do," Omar said.

"That's what dads do."

Omar turned over and stared up at the ceiling. "You know what? We could just leave."

"Leave? And go where?" Rahim asked.

Omar propped himself up on his elbow.

"Anywhere. You got a *Star Trek* phone. We can literally go anywhere we want."

"It's not a toy. We can't just go anywhere. Every time I use that phone, I'm changing things. Important things. So, no, we can't just use it."

"You're just scared. You just said it was a great concert. We could just type in any place and leave. Go somewhere no one can tell us what to do again."

"And what would we do once we got there? How would we eat? Where would we stay? I've told you the phone ain't magic. It can't make cheeseburgers and hundred-dollar bills. You talking crazy. I'm going to bed," Rahim said.

He unfurled his blankets and lay down.

"We could go anywhere we wanted if you weren't a fraidy-cat," Omar whispered.

Rahim heard him but just barely. He thought about grunting an answer, but as soon as his head hit the pillow, he drifted off to sleep.

24

KASIA PLACED HER TABLET on its swivel stand. She made sure her wireless keyboard was connected through the Wi-Fi while she kept running decryption programs on her desktop computer. The tablet showed footage of the multiple vortexes around Philly. One had popped up in the middle of the ice rink at Dilworth Park. Another one appeared in the middle of Market Street. The one in her backyard was still there, but it had stopped growing.

Her mom and dad had gone out extra early and gotten her some serious upgrades for her equipment to help her get Rahim back and hopefully plug all the holes that were popping up all over the timeline. The morning news was calling it an unprecedented event.

Kasia thought that was what her mom would've called a grand understatement. In addition to the new tablet, she'd gotten a new laptop and a router that looked like the engine of a car.

"Mom, Dad, this is too much," Kasia had said as they unloaded the equipment.

"Button, those time-vortex things are showing up everywhere. This isn't just about Rahim anymore," her dad said.

"You know if those government guys are monitoring my activity, they'll eventually notice all this new equipment," Kasia replied.

"Don't you worry about them. At this point, I trust you to fix this way more than I do the government."

Kasia touched the screen of the laptop sitting to the left of the desktop. The sound of a phone ringing filled the room.

The phone rang and rang.

Come on, Ra. Answer, Kasia thought.

She was close to breaking the encryption on the last satellite. It was quickly becoming a race against time. Could she break the encryption before the government realized it and threw up an even more complicated firewall? She wanted to make sure the phone was fully charged and ready to go when she did.

The ringing stopped abruptly.

"Okay, that's cruddy," Kasia murmured.

Iago appeared outside her window. She had reprogrammed him to fly around the house and keep an eye out for the agents.

She touched the screen and accessed his camera.

It wasn't the agents.

It was Dr. and Mrs. Reynolds. They were at the front door.

Kasia let out a long sigh. Her mom and dad had gone to the co-op. They had let her stay home today so she could keep working on helping Rahim. So it was just her and Iago at the house. She went downstairs and opened the door. Dr. Reynolds was wearing a long black coat. Mrs. Reynolds had on a thick plush sweater.

"Hello, Kasia. Can we talk with you for a moment?" Dr. Reynolds asked.

Kasia nodded.

"We just wanted to ask you—and please understand you're not in any trouble—do you know where Rahim is?"

Kasia bit her bottom lip. "I don't know where he is right now. But I promise as soon as I hear something, I'll let you know."

Mrs. Reynolds wiped her eyes. "We don't care where he's gone. We just want him home. If you are talking to him or communicating with him, please let him know he isn't in trouble. We just want him home."

"So do I, Mrs. Reynolds. So do I," Kasia said. As she spoke, a fire engine screamed down the street. The ground beneath their feet shook for at least five seconds. Dr. Reynolds stumbled to his right and grabbed the railing on the steps. Mrs. Reynolds leaned against the doorjamb. Kasia kept her balance by extending her arms and waving them in small circles. A few of her mother's sculptures fell off the foyer shelf and shattered against the floor.

Finally, the ground stopped shaking.

"Was . . . was that an earthquake? In Philly?" Mrs. Reynolds asked.

"I don't think so." Kasia pointed down the street. The fire truck had come to screeching stop. Blocking its way was what appeared to be an old-fashioned steam-powered locomotive engine. The kind that was popular in the Old West. Kasia knew it was from the Old West because last year she'd built a scale-model train for her history assignment. Behind the engine was the now-familiar wavy vortex. A plume of smoke rose from the chimney of the train engine.

"I really have to get back to my homework," Kasia said.

"Uh-huh," Dr. Reynolds said. He was staring at the train engine.

"If I hear from Rahim, I'll let you know."

"Please do that, Kasia," Mrs. Reynolds said. She was staring at the train engine as well.

Kasia stepped back and closed the door. *We gotta get you back, Rahim, before a T. rex shows up in LOVE Park.*

25

"GET UP!"

Rahim rolled over on his side and opened his eyes.

Ms. Lottie was standing in the bedroom doorway. Her face was drawn, and her mouth was set in a harsh straight line.

"I'm . . . I'm awake. I'm ready to go," Rahim said. He wasn't really ready, but he figured he didn't have a choice.

"Get up! Omar is gone, and I know you know where he went!" Ms. Lottie yelled.

Rahim blinked his eyes. "Wh-what?" he stammered.

Ms. Lottie stepped into the room. "He's gone! I came to wake y'all up for breakfast, and he's gone! Now where did he go?" she said.

Rahim reached for his back pocket. The phone was gone.

Oh no, he thought.

"Ma'am, I don't know. I swear. He was here when

I went to sleep last night," Rahim said. That was true. Omar had gone to bed after Grandpa Sam had scolded them. But now he had the phone and could be anywhere.

"Oh Lord. Oh Lord, have mercy. I gotta call Sam. I gotta call his daddy." Ms. Lottie rushed out of the room and down the stairs.

Rahim put his head in his hands. He felt sick. Omar was gone with Rahim's only way home.

When he raised his head, there was the figure in the metallic-green trench coat and the fencing helmet standing in the doorway. It was holding up four fingers on one hand. The other hand was balled up into a fist.

Rahim closed his eyes and mumbled, "There isn't anyone there. This isn't real. There's just something wrong with your head because of all this time-travel stuff."

He opened his eyes.

The figure was still there, still holding up four fingers and a tightened fist like it was going to punch someone. Suddenly the figure's hand gestures made sense.

"Oh man," Rahim said.

The figure in the trench coat nodded.

Then it disappeared.

It didn't fade away like a spirit. It just vanished. One minute it was in the doorway. The next minute it was gone.

Rahim ran down the stairs.

He walked into the kitchen and saw Ms. Lottie on the phone. Cy was leaning against the fridge. Shaka was sitting at the table.

"I think I might know where he went," Rahim said.

"You really think he's on the bus with this Four the Hard Way group?" Grandpa Sam asked. He was standing in the kitchen with his arms crossed so tightly across his chest Rahim thought his sleeves were going to rip.

"Yes, sir," Rahim said.

"And how did he get on a tour bus?" Ms. Lottie asked.

"I don't know how . . . I'm pretty sure that's where he went." Rahim hated lying, but he didn't think they'd believe that Omar had used his phone to teleport himself onto the bus. Which was exactly what he had done while Rahim had been drooling on his pillow.

Grandpa Sam took a deep breath. "Shaka, you follow these guys. Where's their next show?"

Shaka shrugged. "I don't know. I mean, I knew they were coming to Philly, but that was about it. I didn't really care where else they were going."

"Pittsburgh," Rahim said.

"What?" Grandpa Sam said.

"Their next show after Philly was supposed to be Pittsburgh, but they stop in Spring Run," Rahim said.

Except that wasn't really true anymore, was it? According to the Wikipedia article he'd read about Four the Hard Way, they'd stopped in Spring Run to wait for the Sultan to be released from the hospital after he got hit by a car. But because Omar and Rahim had been at the concert, he didn't get hit, so the group had no reason to stop. So they were probably still on the road.

"Let's go. You and me and Shaka. It's four hours from here to Pittsburgh. With traffic they probably haven't gotten that far." His grandfather pulled out his car keys.

"Me?" Rahim asked.

"You know what the bus looks like, don't you?" he said. "Come on."

"Grandpa Sam, if Omar is on this bus, they will find him and pull over and call us. I don't think they wanna be accused of kidnapping a twelve-year-old," Ms. Lottie said.

"I don't trust these rappers to do the right thing." He growled the word *rappers* like it tasted sour.

"They really aren't bad guys. They're actually kinda nerdy," Rahim said.

"Huh? What are you talking about?" Cy said.

"I mean, when we went on the tour bus, they had comic books all over the place. MC Juice collects *Star Wars* action figures. Rock G reads most of the time. Too Smooth likes kung fu movies and math. Like, he likes math a lot," Rahim said.

"Well, I officially don't like them anymore," Shaka said.

"I don't care how nerdy they are. I can't have my son out there by himself."

"Like Ronald is?" Ms. Lottie said.

"I told you I've made up my mind about that," Grandpa Sam said.

"Weren't you the one who said we couldn't just turn him over to the authorities?" Ms. Lottie said.

"We are not talking about Ronald right now. We have to get Omar back. Come on. Let's go."

"If Omar is on that bus, I hope they are treating him . . . well, just like I'm sure Ronald's people want someone to treat him well," Ms. Lottie said.

"She got ya there, Sam," Cy said.

"We'll talk about this later." Grandpa Sam headed for the door. Shaka got up and lightly thumped Rahim on the arm as he passed him. Rahim fell in line as the three of them walked out the door.

"I figure we get out the city and we can . . ." Grandpa Sam's voice trailed off.

A vortex was swirling across the street from the house. The air inside it rippled like water in a pond after someone had tossed a rock into it.

Short, squat gray-feathered birds with sharp-hooked beaks ran out of the vortex. Six of them crossed the street in a flock and flapped down the sidewalk. They were each about the size of a cocker spaniel.

"Wh-wh-what . . . what . . . ?" Grandpa Sam stammered.

"Dodos," Rahim said.

"Say what?" Shaka said.

"Those are dodo birds. I learned about them in science class."

"Didn't they go extinct, like, three hundred years ago?" Grandpa Sam asked.

"Yes, sir. Yes, they did. Mr. Reynolds, I think before we get on the road I need to tell you something. Kasia said I should keep quiet, but I think it's too late for any of that," Rahim said.

"Does what you have to tell us have to do with Omar?" Grandpa Sam was still staring at the dodos as they alternately harassed and avoided people on the sidewalk.

"Yeah. It's about Omar. It's about me. It's about all of us." Rahim watched as the dodos crossed the street again. "It's about time."

26

"ANSWER THE PHONE," Kasia mumbled.

Iago was sitting on the desk next to her. The police and the fire department were still out in the street trying to move the train engine. She figured the agents wouldn't want to wade through all of that to get to her. Plus, with the temporal instability currently surrounding her house, she kept Iago inside, afraid he might get sucked into a vortex and end up in the Stone Age.

Where was Rahim? Why wasn't he answering the phone? It was just ringing and ringing like a broken doorbell.

"Hello?" a voice said finally.

You're not Rahim, Kasia thought. She grabbed her wireless keyboard and pushed a few keys. A voice-modulating program came online.

"You're not Rahim," Kasia said. The voice that came from her speakers to stretch out across time and space sounded like a robot with a bad cold.

"Uh, no. I'm Omar. I don't know who Rahim is. I've got my friend Ronald's phone."

"Oh, beans and rice!" Kasia said as she sat up straight. Omar was Dr. Reynolds's first name. She spoke very slowly. "Omar, why do you have Ronald's phone?"

She heard what sounded like the roar of a motor.

"Well, see, I wanted to get out of my parents' house. They never let me do anything and—"

"Omar. I'm going to ask you again. Where is Ra—er, I mean Ronald, and why do you have his phone?" Kasia said.

Omar gulped. "I, um, borrowed it. I wanted to go on tour with Four the Hard Way. But now I'm on their bus and stuck in the bathroom and it sounds like they are all arguing and . . . I'm kinda scared," he said. "I didn't really think this through."

"Really? I'm shocked," Kasia deadpanned.

"Who are you?" Omar said. "You're not very nice."

"I don't have time to be nice. The space-time continuum is being ripped apart."

"The what?"

"Never mind. I'm going to assume that you used the phone to teleport yourself onto the bus, right?" Kasia said.

"Uh . . . yeah," Omar said.

"Has anyone seen you?" Kasia asked.

"No, I don't think so."

"Okay. Here's what you're gonna do. You're gonna go home."

"I can't! My dad is gonna kill me!"

Kasia rolled her eyes.

"Gosh, you're just like Rahim. Listen, your dad being angry at you is really the last—and I mean the *last*—thing we need to be worrying about right now. Time itself is being pulled and stretched, and I'm kinda afraid it's gonna crumble like graham crackers dunked in milk. So, you're gonna go home. You're gonna give Ronald his phone back, and you're gonna try to forget all about this, or I'll cut the phone off and leave you trapped on that bus with a bunch of spoiled musicians who will probably drop you at the next intersection."

She couldn't really cut the phone off, but she had to sound scary and official. Truth be told, Rahim's coming home might not stop what they had accidentally put into motion. But if she was being honest right now, she didn't care. She just wanted her friend home and safe.

She could fix the timeline later. But none of that was going to happen if she couldn't persuade the younger version of Dr. Reynolds to go home.

"You really think time is falling apart?" Omar asked.

"I just saw an Old West cowboy train come flying down my street," Kasia said. "I live in North Philly."

Omar didn't say anything for a few seconds, and

then, "Okay. I'll go home. Do you think you could tell my dad about the whole time-stream thing? You know, maybe that will keep him from grounding me until I'm twenty-one."

"Yeah, sure. But you gotta get Ronald his phone back. Like, now. Like, right now. Like, with the quickness," Kasia said.

"Okay, I will," Omar said. "But can I ask you something first?"

"What?" Kasia said.

"Are you and Ronald aliens?"

"Go home, Omar."

"I don't wanna sell our music for a car commercial!" Too Smooth yelled as he opened the bathroom door. There was a kid standing there holding a huge cell phone.

"Hey, you're the kid from last night. What are you doing here? Oh man, did you hide out in here?" Too Smooth said.

"I . . . I wanted to go on the tour," Omar said. Saying it out loud suddenly made him feel very foolish.

"Come out of there, little man. Let's call your parents," Too Smooth said. Omar followed him as they walked toward the front of the bus.

"We got us a stowaway," Too Smooth said. The

Sultan popped his head up and peered over the backrest of his seat.

"Say what? Oh snap, that's little man from last night. Yo, you saved my life," the Sultan said, nodding toward his two cousins. "You a better bodyguard than these two."

"Stanley, tell Roger to pull into the next rest stop so we can get . . . What's your name, man?" Too Smooth asked.

"Omar."

"Yeah, so we can get Omar back to his parents."

"Stop calling me Stanley!" the Sultan said. He got up and walked to the front of the bus to talk to the driver.

"He's hated that name since we was kids. Now, what are you doing here? I know your peeps are probably worried sick," Too Smooth said. He sat down and gestured for Omar to sit down in the seat across the aisle.

"You don't understand," Omar said. "They don't let us do anything fun. My pop is always yelling at us about school and college and working hard. I mean, I like school and I want to go to college, but I want to do other stuff too." He didn't feel that afraid anymore. It was really easy to talk to Too Smooth.

"Yo, I'ma let you in on a secret. I love performing. Being in front of a live crowd, ain't nothing like it for real. And I love meeting people I look up to. Like, we played a show a few weeks ago with Goodie Mob and the Roots. But it ain't always fun. Being on tour can get old. I miss my folks. I miss my friends back home. I miss good food. I miss my bed. I get homesick sometimes," Too Smooth said. He paused for a moment and looked out the window.

"What I'm saying is, this ain't all the fun and games you think it is, little man. Real talk. And I know your pops might seem like he's being tough on you, but that's because he wants the best for you. I promise you that. And you probably done scared him and your mom to death, man."

"Yeah," Omar said. He felt like there was a lump in his throat. The air brakes of the bus let out a long hiss as they slowed down and eased into a rest stop.

"Why don't you give your folks a call and I can tell them where we are, okay?" Too Smooth said.

"Okay. Hey, can I use the bathroom first?" Omar said.

"Weren't you just in there? Nah, I'm just messing with you. Go ahead, man."

Omar got up and walked back to the bathroom. Once inside, he typed his address into the phone and pressed SEND.

"Hey, little man, you all right in there?" Too Smooth asked.

He knocked on the bathroom door. There was no response.

"Hey, Omar, you okay?" Too Smooth grabbed the door handle. It was unlocked. He opened the door.

The bathroom was empty.

Too Smooth closed the door. He went back to his seat and didn't say a word.

"Hey, man, you okay?" the Sultan asked.

"I think I'm gonna need a break. I think we been on the road a little too long."

27

"WE NEED TO CATCH up with the bus," Grandpa Sam said. He started his van. Shaka sat up front; Rahim sat in the back seat. The dodos had disappeared, but a man dressed like a Revolutionary War solider had appeared on the sidewalk carrying a musket and looking incredibly confused as they had piled into the van.

"But what about those birds that came out of that, that—I don't know what to call it—but those birds been extinct for, like, hundreds of years!" Shaka said.

"In school they told us they went extinct because they were too trusting of humans, but they're mean as the geese at your house in Muscle Shoals." Rahim didn't see much point in watching what he said anymore. If his grandfather or Shaka heard him, neither one was in the mood to acknowledge it.

"I can't worry about none of that. We gotta get your brother. That's all that matters." Grandpa Sam started to pull away from the curb.

Rahim felt a strange sensation. The hairs on his arm

stood up like they were charged with static electricity. A bright bluish-white light appeared in front of the van. The light glowed so brightly they all had to shield their eyes as Grandpa Sam slammed on the brakes.

When the light was gone, Omar was standing in front of the van.

Grandpa Sam put the van in park and hopped out with surprising agility. Rahim and Shaka followed him.

"Boy, where were you?! Don't you ever leave and not tell us where you going!" He grabbed Omar and hugged him tight.

"I'm sorry, Pops. I—I was, uh, I—I, um—" Omar stammered.

Rahim stepped up and said, "It's okay to tell them the truth. We just saw a flock of dodos and Paul Revere. No use trying to hide anything anymore."

Omar nodded and pulled the phone out of his pocket. He handed it to Rahim. "I used Ronald's phone to teleport myself to Four the Hard Way's tour bus," Omar said.

His father stared at him for a few seconds with his mouth open before turning to face Rahim.

"Shaka, take your brother in the house. Ronald, get back in the van. I'm taking you to social services right now," he said finally.

"Pops, no, please listen! There was a guy who called

his phone and told me that time is starting to fall apart. We need to help him get back to his own time or time itself might be destroyed!" Omar said.

"We did see some extinct birds and a guy from the Battle of Bunker Hill," Shaka said.

Grandpa Sam shook his head.

"I'll take you to the social services building, but that's all we can do for you. I don't know who you are or where you're really from, but you're dangerous. And I can't have that around my family," he said.

"We can't just leave him there, Pop," Omar pleaded. "That's not right."

"Boy, are you giving me back talk?"

"You always say there are things bigger than us. There are things more important than the feelings of one person. I think this is one of those times," Omar said.

"Ronald, Omar gave you back your phone, right?" his grandfather asked.

"Yes, sir."

"Then we've helped him all we can, Omar. Take your brother in the house, Shaka."

Fifteen minutes later, Grandpa Sam pulled up to the curb in front of a large gray granite building. He stopped the van. Rahim opened the sliding door and got out.

Grandpa Sam rolled down the passenger window.

"I wish you luck, son. You seem like a nice boy. But I can't have this craziness around my sons. You understand that, right?"

"I get it. My dad would do the same thing," Rahim said. Grandpa Sam gave him a little nod before raising the window and pulling away.

Kasia must have used that voice-changing thing on her computer when Omar talked to her, Rahim thought.

"She must have finally fixed it!" Rahim pulled out the phone and scrolled to the most recent call. His finger was millimeters away from the SEND button when—as if on cue—he heard Tyrone's voice behind him.

"You keep showing up and I keep getting in trouble, you little buster," Tyrone said.

Rahim turned slowly. Tyrone was standing ten feet away from him. He didn't have his sidekicks with him this time.

"Cops bring you down here, huh?" Rahim asked.

Tyrone balled up his fist and walked toward Rahim.

"My mama works here," Tyrone growled.

"Oh, my bad," Rahim said.

Tyrone balled up his other fist. "I'm gonna smash you!" he said.

Rahim took off running with Tyrone in pursuit.

He looked over his shoulder. Tyrone was right on his

heels. He could grab Rahim's T-shirt if he stretched his hand out.

Well, this is terrible, Rahim thought right before he slammed into a parking meter.

Rahim fell to the sidewalk. The phone jumped out of his hand and skittered across the concrete, stopping right at Tyrone's feet.

"Dropped your fancy phone, dummy," Tyrone said. He picked it up and turned it over in his hands. "I don't think a loser like you needs this. I'll keep it safe for you."

"Give it back! You don't know what it can do!" Rahim gasped, getting to his feet.

"What, you think I'm stupid? It's a phone. You talk on it," Tyrone said. He started smashing the buttons on the touchscreen. Then mockingly held the phone up to his ear.

"Give it back!" Rahim said.

"Come and get it so I can knock you to the other side of China," Tyrone said.

Both boys turned to look at the green light on the top of the phone as it began to blink.

"Tyrone, did you hit the speaker on the search bar?" Rahim asked.

"The what?" Tyrone said.

A bright and shimmery bluish light surrounded Tyrone.

Then he was gone.

Rahim stood there, his mouth wide-open and his eyes bugging out. Tyrone was gone with Rahim's only way home.

"This can't be happening!" he whispered.

"You better believe it is," said a homeless man, now wearing a blue Hawaiian shirt, pushing a shopping cart as he walked past him.

KASIA WAS UP TO her eyeballs in decrypted code when an alert on her computer started ringing like a fire alarm.

"What in the world?"

The computer linked to Rahim's phone, which was also linked to the satellite network she had pretty much cracked, was beeping and whistling like a teakettle. Kasia clicked a few keys and pulled up the program that she had first used to create the phone.

"That . . . that can't be right," she said.

The phone used a variation of a traditional GPS tracking program. She'd only added it because she was fairly certain Rahim would lose the phone one day and they'd have to track it down. He was always leaving his books in her house. He'd lost his book bag on the train more than once, so she was just being cautious.

When he'd told her he was in the past, she hadn't bothered checking the GPS tracker because, well, GPS wasn't on cell phones in 1997, so she didn't think it would work.

Dang, I'm better than I thought, Kasia thought. Somehow, someway GPS was tracking the phone. Which was good. But where the phone was going was . . . very weird.

"China. Now it's in Pennsylvania. Now it's at the North Pole. Now it's back in Pennsylvania. Now it's back in China. Now it's back at the North Pole. Now China again. Rahim, what are you doing?" Kasia said. Iago landed on her shoulder.

"Yeah, this isn't good, buddy," Kasia said as she stared at the monitor. She opened a separate window and called Rahim.

As the phone rang, a huge roar echoed around her house. She rolled her chair over to the window and took a peek outside.

She hadn't studied dinosaurs a lot, but she was fairly sure a triceratops was walking down the street toward the corner.

"Come on, answer the phone, Rahim. Please."

"Where am I??? Help!!!" a voice said. A voice that wasn't Rahim's. Kasia rolled her eyes before hitting the voice modulator again.

"Where is Rahim?" she asked.

"I don't know! I don't know where I am."

"What do you see? Where is Rahim?" Kasia asked.

"I'm standing on this big wall," the boy said. He started crying.

"Listen carefully. Stop. Breathe. Look at the phone. Hit the microphone icon and say, 'Philadelphia 1997 most recent location,'" Kasia said.

"What?"

"Just do it. And then give the phone back to Rahim," Kasia said.

"Who is Rahim?"

"Do what I tell you and make sure you give phone back to the boy you took it from or you might find yourself in the Middle Ages," Kasia said.

"O-o-okay," he said.

Her computer beeped once. She clicked on the GPS window. The phone was back in Philadelphia.

"Is he there?" Kasia asked.

"Here, take it!" the boy said.

Rahim was still standing by the parking meter with his hands in his pockets. Tyrone suddenly appeared and threw the phone at him. The phone bounced off his chest, but Rahim reached out and juggled it from hand to hand.

"Oops, dang it, come on!" he said.

"Rahim! Are you all right?" Kasia yelled.

Rahim watched helplessly as the phone rotated in the air, missed his fingers by a millimeter, and slammed into the sidewalk. The screen turned into a spiderweb as it cracked. The electric-blue outer casing shattered into pieces. Tyrone took off running.

Rahim picked up the phone, or what was left of it. The green and red lights were blackened like blown-out light bulbs. He turned it over. Without the protective casing, the internal workings of the phone were exposed. He stared down at the shattered remains.

This was it. He was never going home. He was never going to see his mom or his dad or his sister or Kasia again.

In the distance, he heard what sounded like a giant mountain lion growling. He looked up and saw a saber-toothed tiger bounding over the roof of the post office across the street.

OMAR HEARD SOMEONE KNOCKING at the door, but he wasn't sure if he should stop writing his essay about "The Truth and How It Affects Our Lives."

"Now, who is this?" Uncle Cy said. He got up and went to the door.

"Long as it ain't a dodo bird, I think we okay," Shaka said.

Rahim was standing on the doorstep. He was holding the pieces of his phone in his hands.

"Huh, it is a dodo bird," Shaka said.

"Ronald!" Omar said. He got up from the couch and ran to the door.

"What you doing here, boy?" Grandpa Sam said, coming out of the kitchen, holding a cup of coffee.

"I'm in trouble and I need your help," Rahim said.

"Ain't nothing Omar can do for you, son. Close the door, Cy."

"WAIT! Please. It's not just about me. Those birds

you saw. That guy who was dressed like a soldier. The trash can that fell from the sky."

"The World War Two tank at the train station," Shaka offered. His father shot him a look.

"All of it is because of me. Because I'm here. Because of this phone. I'm not as smart as the person who built this phone. She's a genius. But I know it's not a coincidence that all of this is happening at the same time I got here from the future," Rahim said.

"The future? Boy, you really is crazy. Close that door, Cy."

Cy started to shut the door.

"When you were sixteen years old, you took your father's car and went joyriding. You got in a lot of trouble and were heading down the wrong path, but you were able to change. You went to work for a guy who was an electrician and a plumber. I think that's why you're so hard on Omar and Shaka," Rahim said. The old story his grandfather had told him came out in one long sentence. Sitting on his grandparents' porch in Muscle Shoals, Rahim thought the story had sounded fun and exciting. Now he realized how much it had affected his grandfather and his own father.

Grandpa Sam almost dropped his coffee cup.

"How do you know that? Did Cy tell you?"

"Me? Nuh-uh. I ain't really been talking to the little fella," Cy said.

"I know it because I know you in the future. Kasia told me not to talk about it, but I think we are way past that stage now. It's like when you gotta sacrifice your queen to get the king out of check," Rahim said.

"Pop, you gotta help him. He sacrificed his queen," Omar said.

"Who's the queen?" Cy asked.

Grandpa Sam walked to the door.

A single-propeller plane streaked by overhead, just barely missing the tops of the row houses across the street. Rahim craned his neck just in time to see the words SPIRIT OF ST. LOUIS on the plane's nose. When he looked back toward his grandfather, he was looking at him with his hands on his hips. His eyes moved from the pieces of plastic in Rahim's hands to Rahim's pleading face. He looked at Omar and Shaka and Cy. Finally, his gaze settled on Rahim again.

"What do you need me to do?" Grandpa Sam asked.

"Can you fix it?" Rahim said. He placed the pieces of the phone in his grandfather's wide, callused hands.

"Shaka, get my soldering kit out of the van," Grandpa Sam said.

Rahim and Omar sat on the couch as Grandpa Sam and Shaka worked on the phone at the kitchen table. The smell of melted plastic and burning metal filled the house. Cy sat in the recliner and flipped through channels with the television remote.

"A wagon train just showed up at the Spectrum," Cy yelled into the kitchen.

"All right, you gotta tell me. How do you know my pop in the future?" Omar asked.

Rahim scratched his head. "It's complicated," he said.

"It can't be more complicated than a super phone that bends time and space," Omar said.

"Trust me, it is," Rahim said.

"Okay, do we know each other in the future?"

"Yeah, you could say that," Rahim said.

"Man, stop playing. Tell me something cool."

Rahim frowned. "Everybody has the internet in their phones. You don't have to go to the library or your desktop computer to get online. I mean, I still go to the library, but I like real books," he said.

"I said tell me something cool."

"It's cooler than you think," Rahim said.

"I think it's fixed," Grandpa Sam called.

Rahim and Omar stood up from the couch as he came into the living room. He handed the phone to Rahim.

"I replaced the screen with tempered glass with a clear

coat on it. I reconnected the circuits and put the casing back together. Replaced the bulbs on top too. I did the best I could. I've never seen some of the stuff in that phone," he said.

Rahim touched the POWER button.

Nothing happened.

No one said anything for a long time.

Finally, Cy spoke. "Maybe you gotta hold it down."

"Yeah," Rahim said.

He held the POWER button down for a few seconds.

The green and red lights on the top of the casing began to flash. All the icons on the touchscreen blinked a few times as the phone powered up.

"My pop can fix anything," Omar said.

His father smiled at him.

"Thank you, Mr. Reynolds. I appreciate your help. I'm sorry I caused all this trouble," Rahim said.

"No, I'm sorry, Ronald. This situation is way more complicated than I thought. And it wasn't okay for me to blame you for anything Omar did. I'm hard on my boys and I pride myself on teaching them right from wrong. And it's wrong to blame somebody else for their actions. Doing the right thing is a choice. And everybody makes that choice for themselves," he said.

"I guess there's nothing left to do but call my friend

and see if she's fixed things so I can go home," Rahim said. He pressed the CALL button and held the phone to his ear.

Kasia was taking a nap on the couch next to her mom when she heard the incoming call alert on her computer.

"That's Rahim!" Kasia said. She jumped up and made a beeline for the stairs. Just as she put her foot on the bottom step, someone started pounding on their front door.

"Who in their right mind is on the street now? The governor told everyone to stay home after that cop car got run over by that stagecoach," her dad said. He got up from the couch and went to the door. When he opened it, Agent Green and Agent Brown were standing there, looking a little worse for wear.

Their suits were torn and frayed in multiple places. Agent Green's tie had been sliced off below the knot. Agent Brown's tie was completely gone, and both men were covered head to toe in what appeared to be soot and mud.

"Hello, Mr. Collins. We need to speak with Kasia," Agent Brown said.

"What in the world happened to you two?"

"Genghis Khan attacked our office. Luckily, some woolly mammoths were able to cut him off at Sixth and Arch," Agent Green said.

"I see," Dad said.

"You guys look terrible," Kasia said.

Agent Brown nodded. "Yes, well, we've been fighting to keep Temüjin from overrunning our office."

"The way things have been going, I don't think you're joking," Dad said.

"Trust me, we aren't. Mr. and Mrs. Collins, we're not here to harass you. We're not here to intimidate you. We are here to ask you and your daughter for your help," Agent Brown said. He turned his attention to Kasia.

"You are one smart lady, Kasia Sierra Collins," he said, and got down on one knee. "Some eighty years ago, our government tried to harness technology they didn't fully understand. Back then, a very smart young lady like you was able to take control of that technology. What you did was wrong," said Agent Brown, "but so was what we did."

"None of that matters now," Agent Green said. "The important thing—the thing that really matters—is that we need your help to close the doors we both had a hand in opening."

"The very nature of reality is warping. If we don't fix it soon, dinosaurs, antique locomotives, and ancient warlords will be the least of our worries. The entire universe may rip itself to shreds. If you and your parents will accompany us to our headquarters, we have the most advanced equipment available. We can help you fix this before it goes too far," Agent Brown said.

A platoon of soldiers wearing Roman legion attire marched in close formation past the front window of the house. Kasia's dad pointed silently at the window. Agent Brown and Agent Green turned their heads just as the last man carrying a spear walked past.

"If it hasn't already," Agent Green said.

Kasia pushed her glasses up on her nose and, turning to her parents, said, "What do you think we should do, Mom? Dad?"

They each gave the other a long, concerned look.

"I think as long as we are with you, it will be okay," her dad said. "We should all have a hand in fixing it."

Mrs. Collins said, "I think there is enough blame to go around about who caused this."

Kasia nodded.

"Okay, I have two requests," she said.

Agent Brown rose to his feet. "And they are?"

Kasia put her hands on her hips. "One—no matter what—I get to bring Rahim home. And two, I won't ever get in trouble for the tiny, eensy-weensy bit of hacking I did to get in your system."

"*Tiny* bit of hacking?" Agent Green raised an eyebrow.

Kasia shrugged.

The house began to tremble. Out the window, they could see a small herd of woolly mammoths being chased by a group of men dressed in animal skins.

"There are mammoths running from some cavemen now," she said.

Agent Brown and Agent Green exchanged a glance.

"We should get going," Agent Brown said.

Kasia thought the computer lab was what her house would look like when she grew up. It was full of state-of-the-art equipment that also looked really, really cool.

There was a whole wall of processors taller than her dad that were ringed in a purple neon light. There were rows upon rows of wide big-screen monitors. People in white coats ran around like mice in a maze as they went from monitor to monitor, checking and rechecking data streams.

Kasia was sitting at one of the 60-inch monitors. They had given her a headset and hooked up her processor to the monitor. A white-coated government scientist was talking to her while taking notes on a tablet.

"How did you solve the spatial displacement equation, though?" she asked.

Kasia pushed her glasses up on her nose. "I didn't really. But by tapping into the wave signal on your

temporal satellite, I was able to piggyback right over that problem."

The scientist nodded furiously as she typed on her tablet. "Fascinating."

Agent Green appeared next to them, wearing a new tie and a change of clothes. "Yes, we are all quite impressed. But can we try to call your friend so we can keep time and space from disintegrating?"

"She reminds me of myself," a whispery voice said. Everyone stopped talking and turned around. Kasia saw an elderly woman in an electric wheelchair at the door of the computer laboratory. She had thick gray hair cut into a large Afro. She wore wide-frame glasses with a pearl chain hooked to the temples. Agent Brown walked with her as she drove her chair over to the desk where Kasia was sitting and held out her hand.

"Dr. Jackson, may I introduce Kasia Collins, our young genius," he said.

Kasia stood, took the woman's hand, and shook it gently.

"Kasia, this is Dr. Evelyn Jackson. She is the director of our division," Agent Brown said.

"I'm also the last living scientist from the experiment that started all this mess, young lady. Of course, back then they didn't allow people like us to put our names on any of the final reports," Dr. Jackson said.

"You . . . you were at the Philadelphia Experiment?" Kasia asked.

Dr. Jackson nodded. "October 28, 1943. Three days before Halloween. That was fitting. I had been part of an all-female civilian welding and electrician unit. They called us the Black Rosies. Six months before they flipped the switch on the experiment, we were moved from our regular assignments in the yard to this top-secret mission that they said could turn the tide of the war. When they found out me and a few others in our unit were actually really good with numbers, they put us inside the lab and had us check and double-check the equations the scientists were using while the scientists were safe

on the other side of the yard," she said. She squeezed Kasia's hand.

"We told them that their equations were off, but they didn't want to listen to us. Things were . . . different back then for people like us. I can still see that ship, the way it lit up like a glow stick. My Lord, it was like seeing lightning in a bottle, then the bottle melted and re-formed itself. Those poor men on the boat." Dr. Jackson shook her head.

"You see, they were trying to make the boat invisible. But what they really did was teleport it backward and forward through time. Tore the ship apart on a molecular level, then snapped it back together. It was . . . terrifying. Those scientists never admitted their mistake. But for some seventy-nine years, they have been chasing that mistake, trying to bend it to their will. After the war, I got married, raised a family, and went back to college. When I got my PhD in physics, the government came calling to ask me to help them fix that mistake. See, they decided they finally wanted to listen to me," Dr. Jackson said as she gave Agents Brown and Green a quick glance.

"And now they've come calling for you. You did something a team of scientists and engineers working for nearly a century couldn't. You sent your friend back in time. Safely. Yet that very act has destabilized reality. So,

I've come down out of my very comfy office to learn how you did it and make sure no one ever does it again. Human beings are remarkable creatures, but we can also be greedy. I don't think time travel is something we need to possess. Do you, Kasia?" Dr. Jackson asked. Agents Brown and Green looked down at the floor. The other scientists in the laboratory busied themselves with their equations.

"No, ma'am. It's too dangerous," Kasia said.

"Smart girl," Dr. Jackson said.

"Are you . . . are you gonna get in trouble if we fix it and nobody can use it again?" Kasia asked.

Dr. Jackson laughed. "No, I'm too old and I've been here too long. And I know too much," she said. Then she winked at Kasia. Kasia smiled.

"Now, if I understand the equations you and my fine folks here have been working on, bringing your friend back should reset everything correctly?" Dr. Jackson said.

"Yeah—I mean yes, ma'am. I think so," Kasia said. "His name is Rahim, ma'am."

"Then let's make that call to Rahim. I'll take care of the rest," Dr. Jackson said.

"Right. Should be easy to get him home now since I don't have to break into the system. Again," Kasia said. She pressed ENTER and his phone began to ring in her headset and from the monitor speakers. Everyone in the laboratory collectively held their breath.

Kasia raised her head and saw the strange person from the alley again, now standing in the far corner of the lab. This time the person was wearing a bright yellow jacket and a pair of red pants, yellow gloves, and shiny black boots. The black helmet had been replaced with a red one. The person seemed to be nodding toward her.

Kasia cut her eyes right to left. No one else noticed the person in the helmet. Kasia was about to ask her mom if she saw anyone when Rahim answered the phone.

"Kasia? I was just about to call you," Rahim said.

"I'm so glad it's you answering your phone."

"Who else would it be?"

"Seriously, Ra? How many times have you lost this phone?"

Agent Green cleared his throat and pointed at his wristwatch.

"Oh yeah. You can come home now."

"What? Why didn't you say that first?"

"I'm saying it now, bighead. Now get back here. You are not gonna believe where I am."

Rahim walked to the front door. He turned and looked at his dad, er, Omar. His uncle Shaka and his grandfather. The three of them were standing in the middle of the living room. Grandpa Sam had his arm around each of his sons.

"I guess this is it. Thank you all for letting me crash here," Rahim said.

"Be safe, son," Grandpa Sam said.

"Later," Shaka said.

"Wait, before you go, tell me, do I become a famous rapper?" Omar asked.

Mr. Reynolds frowned.

"Don't ever give up on your dreams, Omar," Rahim said. It was something his dad would say to him. After a long speech about personal responsibility.

"Hey, who wins the Super Bowl next year?" Cy asked.

Rahim laughed. "Y'all be good." He typed his address and the current year into the search bar. Then he pushed the little magnifying glass icon.

The world around him began to shimmer as a halo of bluish-white light enveloped him. He felt the familiar floating sensation and shut his eyes tight.

Then he was gone.

"Man, I wish he'd told me who won the Super Bowl," Cy said wistfully.

30

RAHIM FELT LIKE HE was falling. He opened his eyes.

A few years ago, his dad had taken the whole family to see a 3D movie. The images created by the cheap plastic glasses were cool, but Rahim had expected to feel like he was actually in the movie.

That was how he felt now. Like he was *in* a movie. Except this movie was the entire history of the universe, and it was set to run at three times the regular speed. He saw lumps of rock swirling around stars and becoming planets. Comets streaked through the solar system. He saw the moon and the earth begin their long dance. He watched as mountains rose and fell. He saw the pyramids being built and the Zulus marching across what would become South Africa. He saw all this and more. More than he could understand. The sensation of falling strengthened, and he closed his eyes.

Then, suddenly, he stopped falling. He opened his eyes again.

He was standing on the front step of his house—

224 St. Albans Street—not a burned-out husk. The cold February air whipped around him and searched for openings in his wardrobe. The streetlamps were just beginning to glow. The sun had set, and the neighborhood was quiet.

Rahim put his hand on the doorknob.

"I'm home. I'm really home," he said.

He turned the knob and opened the door.

He stepped inside and shut the door behind him.

The first thing he noticed was the house was brighter than he remembered. There were two big floor lamps in each corner of the living room that were glowing like a couple of lighthouses.

The next thing he noticed was his dad's bookcase was missing. As was his recliner. Then he saw something that really took his breath away.

"No way!" he said.

There was a huge 72-inch flat-screen television on the wall where the bookcase used to reside. On a coffee table in front of the television were three different gaming systems. He recognized two of them. The third looked like a mash-up of the other two.

Rahim walked over to the TV. A gaming chair was off to the left of it, and there was a beanbag on the other side.

"This isn't right," he said.

"Hey, bighead."

Rahim spun around.

Yasmine was standing in the middle of the living room eating a bag of chips. Her wild Afro seemed to be floating around her face.

"Why are you eating potato chips?" Rahim asked.

"Uh, because I'm hungry. Duh."

"What about your voice? You always saying too much salt is bad for your vocal cords," Rahim said.

"Boy, have you hit your head? I can't sing. Daddy and Mama been looking for you. I'm gonna be late for work. If I was you, I'd come up with a good excuse before they get home." She picked up a smock and grabbed her coat before heading out the door. Rahim saw the name of a local convenience store on the back of the smock.

"See ya later, bighead," she said before walking out the door.

Rahim couldn't make his mouth work, so he just waved. When Yasmine shut the door behind her, he snapped out of his trance. He made for his room, taking the stairs two at a time.

"This is definitely not right," he said when he opened the door to his room.

There was a flat-screen television in his room, too. It wasn't as big as the one in the living room, but it was still pretty big. There was a laptop on his desk and a tablet. In the corner was a keyboard and a digital drum machine.

On his wall were posters of several different groups, but Rahim didn't recognize any of them. His Four the Hard Way poster was missing.

Rahim slowly backed out of the room.

"What is even happening right now?" he whispered. He leaned against the wall. His head was swimming. He began to feel nauseous.

He heard the front door slam.

His parents. That had to be his parents. He swallowed down his nausea and ran down the stairs.

"Stop running, homie," his dad said.

Rahim stopped so suddenly his foot froze in midair. The person speaking to him sounded like his father, but he didn't look anything like the father Rahim knew.

The man in front of Rahim had long black-and-gray dreadlocks. He was wearing a thick Sixers sweatshirt and baggy jeans. On his feet were not his father's leather loafers but a pair of pretty fly Jordans.

Standing next to his father was his mother, but she looked totally different too. Her hair was pulled back into a severe bun. She had on a blazer and pair of khakis. Her usual flowing sarongs and robes were nowhere to be seen. But her smile was the same. "Rahim, where have you been? We've been looking for you for hours," she said.

"Hours?" Rahim asked.

"Yeah, home skillet. We been trying to track you down

for a minute. Your mom been mad worried," his dad said.

"You were worried too, Omar. Stop trying to play it off now," his mom said. She punched his dad playfully in the arm. He pretended to crumple with pain.

"I . . . ugh . . . ," his dad play-gasped.

"We're just glad you're home. We were both worried. Come here, boy," his mother said. Rahim went to her, and she gave him a tight hug. "Now I gotta get to my meeting at the bank before I'm late. Try not to disappear again before I get home, okay?"

"The bank?" Rahim asked.

"You all right, home skillet?" His dad pulled him into a tight half hug.

"I'm just . . . just tired. I went to the library to look up something for a paper," Rahim said. The words came out in one long jumble.

"For four hours?" his father said.

"I'm, uh, really into that paper," Rahim said.

His mother laughed.

"Next time, give one of us a call, please? I know you're growing up, but we need to know where you are, okay?" she said.

"Yes, Mom. I'm sorry," Rahim said.

"All right. I'm gonna go back to the studio. I've been working on this new song. Stanley said if it's as good as I say it is, he'll work it into their set," his dad said.

"Well, don't let anyone hear it before I do. Let me listen to it when I get home tonight, okay?" his mom said. She gave his dad a kiss on the cheek and was out the door before Rahim could say another word.

"Your mama is the best woman I know. Sometimes I think she believes in me more than I believe in myself. Hey, you wanna come down to the studio and listen to this sick new beat I made? It's fire, I'm telling you."

Rahim ran his hands over his face.

"When do you have time to make beats? You teach four classes a day," Rahim said.

His dad laughed. "You sure you okay? Come on, let's go to the basement. This beat is righteous."

"When did we get a studio in the basement?" Rahim said under his breath.

The basement in question was completely reconfigured. There was even a soundproof plexiglass recording booth and a soundboard. Rahim's dad sat at the board and opened a laptop. "Check this out!" he said, and pressed a button. A beat filled the room, and his father bobbed his head in time with it.

Rahim watched, his jaw slack with shock, stunned by what he was hearing.

When it was over, his dad turned around and grinned

at Rahim. "Well, what do you think?" he asked.

I think that was awful. I think that sounded like two cats fighting in a trash can, Rahim thought. But what he said was:

"You made that? Like, you made that all by yourself?"

His dad laughed. "Yep. I'm gonna pass it along to the Sultan and see if they wanna use it for their next album."

"NO!" Rahim yelled.

"What?"

Rahim shook his head. "I mean . . . I mean, how are you going to get it to th-the Sultan?" he asked.

His dad got up and put his hand on Rahim's forehead. "Real talk, son. Are you sure you're all right? You know I work for Four the Hard Way. I've been a roadie for them for years now."

"Say what? How did that happen?"

"I've told you that story dozens of times."

Rahim swallowed hard. "Can I hear it again, please?" he squeaked.

His dad sat back down. "Okay. When I was about your age, me and this guy I knew snuck into a Four the Hard Way concert. After the concert was over, we saved the Sultan from getting hit by a car. He invited us on the tour bus. A few years later, after my friend left town, I ran away from home and hooked up with Four the Hard Way. I became a stagehand and been working for them ever since. I mean, we don't play the big venues anymore, but it's a living. Plus, it gives me time to make my own beats and upload my own songs when I'm not on the road. And one of these days, one of my songs is gonna blow up!" his dad said.

"You never gave up on your dreams," Rahim said.

"Yep! That's what my buddy told me. He was one of the best friends I ever had. You know I almost named you after him. Hey, you wanna hear some new lyrics I came up with? I got them on this thumb drive. Hang on, let me pull them up." His dad spun back around and started fiddling with his laptop.

"Yeah, that would be great." Rahim sighed.

Later, up in his room, Rahim realized why his dad's lyrics were as bad as his beats. They were pretty much the same type of rhymes he'd written when Rahim had been hanging out with him in the past. For a twelve-year-old, they had been pretty good. For a grown man? Not so much.

Rahim lay down on his bed, and something hard dug into his leg. His phone! He sat straight up. He'd almost forgotten he had it. He pulled it out and called Kasia. After a few rings, she answered.

"I forgot to tell you that you can download different ring tones. I just put that generic one on there until you get something you actually like," Kasia said.

"K, I'm gonna ask you a question and it's going to sound crazy, but just ride with me for a minute, okay?" Rahim said.

"Oooh, this sounds good. Go ahead."

Rahim inhaled. "Do you remember me going back in time and you saying that I might mess up the timeline if I talked to anybody?" He swallowed hard. "I think I really messed up the timeline, like really bad."

Kasia didn't say anything for a full minute.

"Kasia? You there?"

"Well, this explains a lot," she said finally.

"Wait, what does that mean?" Rahim asked.

"I've got a ton of files on my computer—stored in a data cloud—all about you going back in time because I hacked a government satellite system. I don't remember any of it. But it must have happened because here you are talking about it," Kasia said.

"It did happen, and it changed everything. My parents are not my parents. I mean, they are, but they are totally different. And I bet it's not just my parents. What do your parents do for a living?" Rahim asked.

"I wanna say you already know this, but since it seems like you're an amateur time traveler, I'm gonna tell you anyway. My mom and dad are both performance artists who use fruits and vegetables in their shows."

"Umm?" Rahim said.

"My grandparents help us pay our bills," Kasia said.

"Oh man. I really messed everything up."

"Look, it's late and I gotta get ready for school tomorrow. And so do you," she said.

"We go to the same school now?" he said.

"Gonna just ignore that, but yeah."

"Are we in the same classes?"

"No. I take accelerated courses," Kasia said. "We're both in chess club, though."

"Well, at least you're still a genius," Rahim said.

"I don't think even you could mess that up. Let me ask you something. Let's go with the idea that you did change things. Are they really that bad? Like, is this reality worse than the one you remember?"

"Have you heard my dad rapping?"

"Yeah, he's awful."

"In the reality I remember, he's a college professor," he said.

"Oof, that's definitely different."

Rahim heard someone in the background talking to her.

"Yes, my maternal unit, I am about to partake of my slumber," Kasia said. To Rahim, "I gotta go to bed."

"Does everyone talk like that now?" Rahim asked.

"Everyone from North Philly does. See you tomorrow."

RAHIM PUT ON HIS book bag and went outside to wait for Kasia. The temperature had risen overnight from completely frigid to regular cold.

Kasia bounded out the house with a backpack emblazoned with several different anime characters and wearing a black hat with cat ears attached to it.

"All right, tell me what I'm like in your original timeline," Kasia said as they headed down the sidewalk.

"Pretty much the same, except you're not into anime."

Kasia blew air over her lips and stuck out her tongue.

"That sounds ridiculous. I love anime. We binge-watch it all the time," she said. They reached the corner and waited for the WALK sign. While they were waiting, a man coming from the opposite direction was trying to shoo away a dodo bird that was following him.

"Is that . . . a dodo?" Rahim asked.

"Yeah. My mom said everyone assumed they went extinct hundreds of years ago, but then a bunch of them showed up when she was a kid here in Philly. My dad says they are worse than pigeons and rats. Hold on a minute. Did you have something to do with that?" Kasia asked.

"I don't even wanna think about it," he said.

Rahim and Kasia went their separate ways when they got to school.

"I'll catch up with you at lunch," Kasia said.

"Yeah, hopefully Demarcus doesn't steal it from me," Rahim said.

"Why would Demarcus steal your lunch?" Kasia asked.

"Uh, because him and his sidekicks hate my guts and want to make my life miserable because my song got more likes than his that time?" Rahim said.

"What song?" Kasia asked.

Rahim slumped against the wall next to a row of lockers. "Don't tell me that you and me don't make songs anymore?"

Kasia frowned. "We've never made songs. Man, your original timeline sounds really interesting. I gotta go."

"Yeah. See you at lunch, I guess," Rahim said.

"That's right, Jerome, the president is elected for one twelve-year term. Now, who can tell me how many times a senator has to fight an opponent in a trial by combat before he or she is reelected?"

Rahim sat in the back of his social studies class hiding behind his tablet as Dayna Givens gave the correct answer to Mrs. Walsh's question. He was beginning to think he hadn't returned to a different timeline. This felt like a different world.

His tablet beeped.

"Okay, everyone, it's time for our sponsorship moment. Repeat after me: 'Global Consolidated Technologies is the world's leading source for educational products,'" Mrs. Walsh said.

"This can't be happening," Rahim mumbled.

"You better believe it is," the janitor said as he passed by the door. Rahim's head snapped up as he glanced to his left. The janitor looked very familiar.

He made it home, but home wasn't his home anymore. They'd stopped the timeline from falling apart and causing the end of all existence, and that was great. It was fantastic. But . . .

This timeline was awful. It was really, really awful.

Lunch couldn't come soon enough for Rahim. He saw Kasia sitting with Harris and Dayna and a kid with a faux-hawk. He headed over with his tray and sat down next to Kasia.

"So, I got fifty points on my Click-Clack account. I'm gonna trade them in for some new Jordans," the boy with the faux-hawk said as Rahim sat down.

"Click-Clack?" Rahim said. The boy stared at him quizzically.

"Yeah, Click-Clack. My last video got over five hundred likes in one hour. Got me fifty points."

"Rahim, you know that you can trade Click-Clack points like money," Kasia said. She gave him a slight wink.

Rahim just nodded. This was just another weird thing that he didn't really understand. Another thing he and Kasia had caused accidentally.

"Oh man, here comes Demarcus," the faux-hawk kid said.

Rahim saw Demarcus walk past them carrying his lunch tray. Rahim couldn't help but notice he looked different. He walked with his head down and his shoulders slumped. His two sidekicks were nowhere to be seen.

"He's so strange," one of the girls said.

"He can't help it. How would you feel if your dad told everybody who would listen that aliens abducted him when he was a kid and teleported him from Philly to ancient China? Then he went on that *Ancient Aliens* show and flipped out," Kasia said.

"I hear his dad goes down to the park and tries to contact UFOs on the weekends," Harris said.

Rahim stared down at his pizza and Tater Tots.

Kasia was waiting for him at the end of the day when the last bell rang. They walked in silence for a couple of blocks until finally Rahim said, "I've been thinking about this all day. The way things are, the way the world is right now? It's not right. My timeline wasn't perfect, but this . . . this is terrible."

"You know I can't really say if you're wrong or right. But I read some of my data files again last night, and your timeline doesn't have rabid dodo birds," Kasia said.

"I think I know what I need to do," Rahim said.

They had reached his stoop. Kasia adjusted her backpack. Rahim sat down on the cold concrete step. Neither one of them said anything for a long time.

Finally, Kasia let out a deep breath. "Let me guess. You want to go back."

"Not just that. I wanna make sure things go back to the way they used to be. Not just for my sister or my mom or dad. For everybody," Rahim said. "Even Demarcus."

32

"OKAY, SO LET'S GO over it again," Kasia said.

Rahim couldn't get over how different her room looked. She still had a ton of computer equipment that Rahim didn't even pretend to be able to operate, but her room was also decked out in LED anime posters and a shelf full of action figures.

"He . . . doesn't get it," Iago said. His voice had a flat mechanical tone.

"In my timeline he doesn't talk," Rahim said.

"Why would I build a drone that can fly, walk, and do complex calculations and not make it talk? That part of your timeline is way, way cruddy," Kasia said.

"I got it, okay. I know this is gonna work," Rahim said. He was sitting on a stool in Kasia's room. The setting sun was casting odd shadows all around the room.

Kasia was at her computer desk. "Listen, we are kinda playing with some really big toys here. Now, I'm still linked into the tri-satellite network. But if you go back, the government may notice and just shut them down. I know you said they didn't do it before, but you going backward and forward in time has changed everything," Kasia said.

"Butterfly effect, right? One little thing has a huge effect on everything else. I got it," Rahim said.

"No, you don't. You just wanna go so you can try to fix things. But there is the very real possibility you could make things worse if you go back to the wrong point in the past and your actions create another timeline that's different from this one or your original one. You could get stuck in a time vortex. A never-ending loop where you bounce from the beginning of the universe to the end and back again. Forever," Kasia said.

Rahim thought of the images he'd seen when he left 1997. The high-speed movie that he had been a part of as he traveled home. What would it be like to be trapped in that movie forever? Floating from the beginning of time to the end and back again?

A shiver went through his body. "Thanks. That didn't scare me at all," he said.

"I'm just trying to keep it real with you. You could be stuck in the past. If you do come back to the present, we might be ruled by lizard people. Or you could slip between timelines and be lost. I don't know what could happen. That's all I'm saying."

"What are the odds I succeed, Iago?" Rahim asked.

The drone whirred and buzzed for a few seconds. "The probability of your returning the timeline to its previous setting has a seventy-eight percent—"

"See, that's good!" Rahim said.

"—risk of failure," Iago said.

"Oh."

"You don't have to do this, you know," Kasia said. "You could just learn to deal with this timeline. I saw on the news that this summer much smaller swarms of giant murder hornets are expected than ever before."

Rahim stood up and pulled out his phone. "I'm going."

"Okay. And you're sure about the destination?" Kasia said.

"Yeah. I think that's the right place and right time. Everything that happened with my dad happened because of that night. I got a feeling if I set that right, everything else will fall into place."

"Oh, you have a feeling. That's great. Really, I'm sure this will not end horribly," Kasia said.

"Just make sure you track me with that GPS thingy, K."

She swiveled in her chair and started typing on her wireless keyboard. "Engaging thingy," Kasia said.

Rahim shook his head. "All right, here we go." He typed in the time, date, and location of his destination.

Kasia spun her chair again and faced him. "Hey, be careful, okay? I don't know how things are in your time-line, but here you're my best friend. I would kinda like it if you made it back in one piece, okay?"

"I will. Just keep track of me and don't get locked out of the network or whatever. And we're best friends in my timeline too," he said. "All right, here we go." He pressed ENTER.

Once the shimmering light around him had dimmed and the sensation of floating had stopped, he took a step back and leaned on a mailbox.

"Time traveling is starting to mess with my stomach," Rahim muttered. The crowd from the concert was spilling out of the hall. The Four the Hard Way bus was parked along the side of the building. It was rapidly being surrounded by the crowd.

Rahim watched as two figures ran around the corner to the bus. One of the figures was Omar. The other was Rahim.

Kasia had said to him: "I don't know what will happen if you talk to yourself in the past. Theoretically you should be okay. It's not like a movie where you would blow up or anything. At least I don't think so. I mean, you're from another separate timeline, so there shouldn't be a paradox."

"Don't blow up. Got it," Rahim had said.

His plan was to somehow prevent his dad and his other self from stopping the Sultan getting hit by the car and breaking his leg, which would in turn keep his dad and his other self off the tour bus. That should keep his dad on the right track to becoming a really good professor instead of a really awful rapper.

At least that's what he hoped would happen.

Rahim watched as his dad and his other self stood back from the crowd and as the members of the group exited through the rear door to thunderous applause. He stepped off the sidewalk and waited for the car to come flying down the street.

"Any minute now."

The crowd erupted into another round of applause and cheers. The Sultan was walking out the door.

Rahim saw the headlights of the car come careening down the street.

He pulled out his phone and dialed his own number. He watched as the other Rahim pulled out his phone, stared down at it, then answered, "Hello?"

"Move to the other side of the street right now."

"Huh?"

"If you don't want your dad to grow up to be the worst rapper in the history of hip-hop, do it now!" Rahim said. His other self frowned as he stepped off the sidewalk.

The car ran up on the sidewalk on the driver's side, then overcorrected to the right. It was no longer headed for the Sultan. It was heading straight for his dad.

"MOVE!" Rahim yelled into the phone.

His other self raised his head just in time to see the car barreling right at him and Omar. Showing reflexes Rahim didn't realize he had, his other self pulled Omar out the way of the car. The two of them tumbled to the sidewalk. People scrambled as the car's brakes screeched, and it came to rest just inches away from the Sultan.

Rahim ran across the street. He remembered what Kasia had said, but he couldn't help himself. He had to make sure his dad was okay.

"Are you all right?" he said. Omar was lying on top of the other Rahim. He got to his feet, brushed off his pants, and adjusted his tie.

"You saved my life, Ronald!" Omar said, extending his hand.

"You're welcome," they both said in unison. The

other Rahim got up off the ground. He had a small cut on his hand, but otherwise he seemed okay.

"You have a twin brother?" Omar said.

"I—"

"Hi, I'm Reginald. Could I talk to my brother for a minute alone?" Rahim said.

"Uh-oh," his other self said. He was staring at the ground.

Rahim looked down, but he didn't see anything. "What are you looking at?" he asked.

"My phone. I dropped it when we fell. I think it went down there." He pointed at a storm drain.

Rahim smacked himself in the forehead. "Are you serious?"

His other self didn't respond.

"You lost the magic phone? How are we gonna get back in the house?" Omar said.

"Never mind that. How am I gonna get home?" Rahim's other self said.

Rahim/Reginald pulled out *his* phone. "You have to go back. You have to go back right now and you have to get rid of this phone."

"What?" his other self said.

"This is how we make everything right."

"If I go back, what's gonna happen to you?" Rahim/Ronald said.

"Go back to the day before you got the phone. Stop Kasia from giving it to us. Then get rid of this one. I think that will make it so that I never came here. I'm thinking it's gonna reset everything." He handed his other self the phone.

"I don't know. I feel like I'm leaving myself behind," Rahim/Ronald said.

"Trust me on this. Things are really bad back home. This is the only way," Rahim/Reginald said.

Omar was looking worried. "What about me? How am I gonna get home?"

"If he does what I tell him to do, it will all work out," Rahim/Reginald said. And turning to his other self: "Do it. Do it before something else happens and we're both stuck here."

Rahim/Ronald looked at Rahim/Reginald, then at Omar. "It was fun hanging out with you. You should follow—"

Rahim/Reginald held up his hand and said, "Nope, don't say that."

His other self shrugged. "Okay. Here goes nothing." He entered his address and the date he wanted to arrive.

Then he pressed ENTER.

A bright bluish-white light began to envelop his other self.

It also enveloped Rahim.

He wasn't in the movie this time. He was floating through what seemed like a cloud of light. Red, green, purple, blue lights. Rahim could hear voices in the light. His father, his mother. His grandfather, his grandmother. Kasia. His sister. Then he was falling down into an illuminated tunnel. He wanted to scream, but he couldn't make a sound.

Something was gripping his right hand. He turned his head. Not something. Someone. The figure in the fencing helmet. Someone else was grabbing his left arm. He didn't recognize them, but they were wearing a similar helmet to the person on his right. The two figures raised their free arms and pointed them upward. Rahim felt his descent slowing. The sensation of falling was replaced by the feeling of ascension. The multicolored cloud became blindingly bright. Rahim couldn't see anything but the light as it surrounded him.

I hope we fixed things. Even if I don't make it home, I hope we made things right, he thought.

Then everything went black.

Rahim opened his eyes.

He was back in his room. His *real* room. He was lying

on his bed. His book bag was in the corner. He got up and looked out his window. The sky was overcast and the window felt cold.

Please let it have worked, Rahim thought. He ran downstairs to the living room.

"We don't run in this house," his father said. He was in his recliner reading a book.

"Sorry, Dad." He walked over to his father and wrapped his arms around him.

"What is this show of affection for? I don't mind it, but I have work to do, Rahim."

"I wanted to let you know I'm so glad you didn't become a rapper," Rahim said.

His father was staring at him. "Okay. That's a bit of an unusual statement, but all right. I mean, once upon a time, I enjoyed the odd rap album," Dad said.

Rahim hugged his dad again. "Dad, would you be mad if I said that I wanted to be a famous rapper?" he asked.

His father closed his book. "Rahim, I'm your father. I'll support you no matter what you want to do. If that means you want to be a rapper, then that means I'll support you. However, that also means you'll get a degree in music theory or sound engineering."

"So I have something to fall back on, right."

"No. So that you have the tools to give yourself the best chance to succeed."

"That's a good idea, Dad. Can I go see Kasia now?" Rahim asked.

"Why? You want to use her computers?" he said.

"No. She's my friend, and I just want to talk to her," Rahim said.

"Have you done your homework?"

"No, but I promise I will do it as soon as I get back. Something big happened at school today and I want to tell her."

"All right. But I'm going to check your homework when it's complete."

"All right. I love you, Dad. I love you just the way you are," Rahim said.

His dad patted Rahim on the head and smiled. "I love you too, son. We'll start talking about colleges with good music programs when you come back. Maybe you and Yasmine can go to the same school?"

Kasia was sitting at her desk. Iago was flying around the room. He landed on her shoulder as she turned to face Rahim. He was holding out the bright blue phone to her.

"You really saw the beginning of time?" Kasia asked.

"And the end. And I saw two people in space helmets who I think saved my life," Rahim said.

Kasia eyes widened. "Were they aliens? Did I solve the problem of time travel and make first contact with an alien civilization?"

"Slow your roll, Stephen Hawking. I don't know who or what they were. The only thing I know is that we need to get rid of this phone," Rahim said. "Take it apart. Grind it up. Whatever."

"Are you sure? I mean, are you really sure that's what you want to do?"

"Trust me, you do not want to get chased by a rabid dodo bird," Rahim said.

"Suit yourself." Kasia touched her tablet. Iago whirred to life and plucked the phone from her hand with his pincers. He flew in lazy circles to the trash can. Then, using his pincers, Iago crushed the phone before dropping it in the trash.

Rahim let out a sigh. "Well, that's the end of that."

"I could rebuild it in the dark with my eyes closed if I wanted to."

"Let's not. I just want things to go back to normal," he said.

"Whatevs. Hey, speaking of normal, you want to go get your notebook so we can work on a song?"

"Why don't we just freestyle and see what happens?"

"Look at you, all fearless and stuff!" Kasia said.

"Oh, one other thing. Can you help me set up an account to start posting my songs?"

"Really?"

"Gotta follow your dreams," Rahim said.

"You know, I've been thinking about something. What do you think about me going to school next year?" Kasia asked.

"I mean, it would be cool having another friend besides Harris. But aren't you, like, way, way past all the stuff we're doing?"

Kasia scrunched up her face. "Yeah, but they have accelerated classes. And I think . . . I wanna get out of this room. Expand my understanding of social dynamics. It's good research."

"Well, I got your back. I don't know how much good that's gonna do with Man Man, but I gotcha," Rahim said.

"I don't know why you're afraid of him," Kasia said.

"He's big, he's mean, and he likes to hurt people. That's all."

Kasia laughed. She spun back around and touched her tablet. A funky beat filled the room. She handed Rahim her wireless mic.

As Rahim was just about to drop a lyric, the lamps in the room began to flicker like strobe lights. Then Kasia's computers and tablets and equipment began to flicker on and off too. Iago landed on the table and shut down with a soft buzz.

"What is going on? I thought we fixed everything by getting rid of that dang phone!" Rahim said.

"I don't know! All my stuff is offline!" Kasia said.

The two figures that had been following them now appeared in Kasia's room. They seemed to glow and were somewhat transparent, and both wore helmets and brightly colored coats. Rahim thought they looked like ghosts.

"Rahim. Kasia. There are forces moving against you. Against the very nature of time itself. Forces that are . . . dangerous. Wheels have been set in motion; bells that can't be un-rung. They want what you created, Kasia, and what you have seen, Rahim. They have kidnapped Dr. Evelyn Jackson and are moving to shape history in their image. We know this sounds frightening, but this is the path you have set upon, and we know you are brave.

"We need your help. Pieces on the board are being manipulated. Pawns are being moved by invisible hands. You, Rahim, and you, Kasia, are the only ones we can trust. The only ones who can help us set things right. Time is like a song. There is a rhythm to it that has been disrupted. If it can't be corrected, all of existence could end in an instant."

The figures spoke in unison. Kasia and Rahim looked at each other, then back at the glowing figures.

"You're holograms!" Kasia said.

"What is going—" Rahim asked.

"We will transmit new schematics for you to build a new, improved time-displacement device. Then, once that has been completed, we will explain everything," the figures said.

"Who are you guys? Who's Dr. Jackson?" Kasia asked.

The figures turned their heads toward each other. Then, without saying a word, they removed their helmets. One of them was a clean-shaven Black man. The other was a Black woman with long, luxuriant braids.

"Dr. Jackson is the key to stopping all this. And we're—" the woman said.

"We're you," the man said.